Snow White
and Ebony

AF220546

Michelle Krabinz

Michelle Krabinz was born in Cologne in 1994 and has been drawn towards the art of writing since her early years of puberty. Even though she wrote a lot of short stories and fairy tales, she never thought about becoming a professional writer until she was in her early twenties.

Since then, she has discovered not only a love for all kinds of art, but also the wish to share her numerous stories and fantastic worlds with other people.

"Snow White and Ebony" tells the story of Snow White and her unplanned twin sister Ebony, the latter of which was born due to the overly rash fulfilment of the queen's wish to have a child with skin as white as snow, lips as red as blood, and hair as black as the ebony wood of her window frame.

As the apprentice fairy of the Good Fairy, who normally grants those wishes, tries her best to fulfil the queen's wish, she gets a little confused about the details and the queen ends up having two daughters instead of one. A mistake with unforeseen consequences for the future of the kingdom …

Trigger warning: This story deals with death and the loss of loved ones. Topics like isolation. depression and loneliness are mentioned.

Michelle Krabinz would like to add that this is a work of fiction. Names, characters, places and incidents either are the product of the author's imagination or are used fictitiously. Any resemblance to actual persons, living or dead, events or localities is entirely coincidental.

Snow White
and Ebony

Michelle Krabinz

An alternative fairy tale

FSC
www.fsc.org
MIX
Papier aus ver-
antwortungsvollen
Quellen
Paper from
responsible sources
FSC® C105338

Die Deutsche Nationalbibliothek verzeichnet diese
Publikation in der Deutschen Nationalbibliografie;
detaillierte bibliografische Daten sind im Internet über
http://dnb.dnb.de
abrufbar.

© 2022 Michelle Krabinz
© 2022 Tiff & Toff - Verlag
Hullenwiesenstraße 8
26316 Varel
Coverdesign: Carmen Schneider –
www.covermanufaktur.art
Lektorat: Hannah Koinig „Lektorat Butterblume"

Herstellung und Verlag:
BoD – Books on Demand, Norderstedt
ISBN: 978-3-7568-8693-7

For my beloved daughter,
Lara Melina,
who taught me
to look at the world
with new eyes

Tiff & Toff Taschenbuch 024

Once upon a time, in a beautiful land filled with woods and rivers, there lived a king and a queen who reigned with great wisdom and kindness.

The king was just and brave, protecting his people from harm and guiding them with wisdom.

The queen was a natural beauty, because she was kind at heart and ate very healthily. She advised her husband in matters of the heart and family quarrels which he had to settle, and he was always glad for her council.

One winter's morning, the queen was sitting beside her window and sewed a gift for her husband. Then she noticed that it had started to snow and looked outside to watch the feathery flakes glide down from the heavens above. Not paying attention to her sewing, her needle slipped and she pricked her finger. Three drops of blood fell into the snow, which had gathered upon the wooden windowsill and as the queen looked upon them, the image of a beautiful child arose before her mind's eye.

"I wish I had a child," she whispered and looked up to the clouds, "with skin as white as snow, lips as red as blood, and hair as black as the ebony wood of my window frame."

She sent her wish to heaven and returned to her sewing, now paying better attention to her fingers so that she wouldn't hurt herself again.

Her wish travelled with the wind, finding its way up into the clouds, where there was a palace made of snow, ice and clouds itself. It was the Cloud Castle of the Good Fairy, who was responsible for making wishes come true. She had been granting wishes for the kingdom for centuries already and had now grown old and tired.

That's why she took in an apprentice, an eager young fairy by the name of Arabella, who was willing to learn that old and powerful magic. She had studied hard for a couple

7

of years and was "getting the hang of it" as she called it herself.

The old Good Fairy trusted her enough to leave her alone from time to time, and so far nothing exciting had ever happened when the Good Fairy had left the Cloud Castle.

All the more surprised was the young fairy apprentice when she suddenly heard the voice of the queen upon the wind, while the Good Fairy was still gone.

"I wish I had a child," sighed the voice of the wind, telling the queen's wish to Arabella, "with skin as white as snow, lips as red as blood, and hair as black as the ebony wood of my window frame."

"Good Heavens!" cried out the young fairy and leapt from her chair. "A wish! And from the queen, too. I'd better wait for the Good Fairy to deal with that. Oh! But what if I forget the details? She always nags how poor my memory is when it comes to specific details. If only I could write! I should tend to that wish right away! Maybe the Good Fairy will be proud of me if she hears that I have managed to grant a wish all on my own."

Filled with joy and excitement, the young fairy unfolded her multi-coloured wings and flew from her room into the Chamber of Wishes. There was a soft mist hanging in the air, like a veil of coloured clouds, which hung above the ground and emanated a scent of sweet dreams.

"Let's see," mumbled Arabella while she skilfully wove her way through the mist, towards the huge shelves which were filled with the ingredients for the wishes.

In the middle of the room was a gigantic cauldron, bigger than the dragonfly-sized fairy herself, filled with clear water, from which the mystical mist was rising up like vapour. Around the cauldron, there were shelves upon shelves, filled with herbs, plants and other ingredients of every colour, taste and scent. Some were dull, other glowing or sparkling, as if light was shining out of their very midst. Among these rows of shelves, the young fairy now started to rummage about, looking for the right ingredients to grant the wish of the queen.

"First, we need something for 'skin as white as snow'. That shouldn't be too hard."

She bustled about the room for a while and added a few things into the cauldron – a few drops of unicorn blood from the 'magical creatures blood donation', some peppermint, pixie dust, ice crystals and a hint of lavender – until the surface looked like it was covered by a layer of glittering snowflakes. Pleased by her work, she turned towards the shelves once more and started to search for the next ingredients.

"So far, so good. Now to the second part of the wish … What was that again? Red as blood … red as blood … But what? The eyes? No! That would look terrifying. Maybe the hair? Yes, why not. Red hair should make for a lovely look, combined with white skin. Redheads are naturally pale anyway. And curls might be nice, too. Always gives things a livelier look."

The young fairy pushed her own silver curls out of her face and went to look for the right ingredients which would fit to her task. She was torn between copper and a truly dark bloody shade of red for a while, but the wish clearly stated the latter, so she added the ingredients to the cauldron.

It was now glowing red as if a tiny sun was hovering under the surface.

"White skin, red hair – now to the last part of the wish. I think it was something about black … Black like ebony wood … Well, skin and hair are already set. Now it would only fit to the eyes. Yes, black eyes might be interesting. Mystical and deep like a starless night or the bottom of a wishing well."

Once more, Arabella bustled about the room, until she had found all the missing ingredients – most important the ebony wood. Finally, she added a few herbs to give the child good health and a sharp mind, before she topped the potion off with a blessing of her own.

"May true love find you and destiny guide you. May you always be just and curious and strong enough to bear the burdens of the life as a –"

She stopped dead and her eyes widened.

"Oh no! I forgot to determine the gender. Wait! Did the queen's wish say anything about that? No, not that I remember … Humph … Kings always like to secure their line with a son. But mothers also like to have girls, so that they aren't surrounded by men all day long. And fathers love daughters as well. A girl it is then."

She quickly added the needed ingredients, stirred the potion once more and finished her blessing:

"– and strong enough to bear the burdens of the life as a princess."

With a look of satisfaction, the young fairy extracted all of the potion from the cauldron with a magical spell and put it into a small crystal vial. With that she flew down into the castle where the king and queen lived and poured it into the soup of the queen when nobody was looking.

Upon her return, the young fairy met the Good Fairy, who was just now getting back into the Cloud Castle herself, her white hair wind-blown from the flight.

"Where have you been?" the Good Fairy asked with an air of suspicion. "Didn't you say you'll watch the castle for me while I'm away?"

"I did and I did – say it and watch it – but I also did grant a wish just now."

The young fairy beamed with pride and nearly couldn't wait to tell her mistress all about it.

"You did grant a wish?" the Good Fairy asked surprised. "What kind of wish?"

"The queen's wish," Arabella answered happily. "She wished for a child and I didn't know when you would get back, so I decided to deal with this one myself. And it turned out pretty nice, I think. The potion was all sparkly and glowing beautifully."

"I see. Tell me all about it then."

The Good Fairy beckoned the young one to follow her into the castle and when she had settled down in her armchair, her young apprentice told her all about the wish, bouncing up and down through the room while she praised her own work.

"– and then I poured it into her soup. Pretty sneaky, right? Nobody saw me, of course! I made sure of that. And I flew straight back to the Cloud Castle, too, just like you always told me."

"Very well," the Good Fairy answered while pondering over the story she had just heard. "And you are sure that the queen asked for a red-headed child?"

"Um … well … My memory might have gotten a bit fuzzy on the details at some point," the young fairy admitted and stopped flying through the room. "But I'm sure there was something about 'red as blood' –"

"Yes, but the hair? Humans these days don't like red hair that much. Some even believe that it is a bad sign and only grows on the heads of witches."

"Oh. I didn't know that –"

"Let's find out then, shall we?"

Arabella looked puzzled, but the Good Fairy just got up from her armchair and flew into the next room, which was called the Chamber of Sight. It was filled by hundreds of mirrors, each showing a different part of the kingdom.

The Good Fairy strode over to one of them which was showing the queen at dinner and waited until her young apprentice had followed her.

"I never told you that," the Good Fairy said, "but if your magic is powerful enough, you can see into the past with those mirrors."

"Seriously??"

The blue eyes of the young fairy widened and she stared upon the mirrors with new awe.

"Yes. And now we shall see if your memory betrayed you or not."

With those words, the Good Fairy waved her hand in front of the mirror and suddenly the image of the queen at dinner vanished. It didn't just disappear though – it started to wind back, faster and faster, until it stopped and showed the queen sitting at the window with an ebony wood frame.

"I wish for a child," the voice of the queen echoed from the past, "with skin as white as snow, lips as red as blood, and hair as black as the ebony wood of my window frame."

A deep silence fell over the room, while they watched the image of the queen fasten forward again, until she was sitting at the dinner table once more.

12

"It's not too late to fix this," the Good Fairy mumbled and suddenly dashed out of the room with an amount of speed that her young apprentice wouldn't have thought possible at this age.

"I'm so sorry," Arabella whined while she followed the Good Fairy into the Chamber of Wishes. "I should have waited for you. If only I had known that I could check on the details again with those mirrors —"

"You wouldn't have been able to do it anyway," the Good Fairy said matter-of-factly, while she was whizzing through the room, picking up ingredients. "You're not strong enough yet. Your magic couldn't do it."

The young fairy watched glumly while the Good Fairy was hurriedly preparing a new potion within the cauldron, which was quickly beginning to show a perfect mix of red, white and black. It was even prettier than the potion of Arabella had been and glowed as bright as a summer's day when the Good Fairy blessed it with the usual attributes — beauty, charm, health — and filled it into one of the crystal vials.

"Now quickly, before dinner is over!"

With that, the Good Fairy flew down to Earth with the speed of lightning and found the queen still sitting at the dinner table, talking to her husband with a cheery voice. The young fairy watched through the mirror and breathed a happy sigh when the potion had found its way into the queen's beverage.

"That was close," the Good Fairy chided her young apprentice as soon as she got back. "Far too close. You're not ready to be trusted with this kind of responsibility yet. Next time, you'll wait for me and prepare the potion under my supervision."

"Yes, mistress. But what is going to happen to the queen now?"

"If all goes as I planned it, she'll have twins. Both girls, but there'll be time for a male heir afterwards. I hope I managed to get things right, because it is important that the girl that I designed gets out first. Fathers often bond with the first-born and that should be the child of their dreams – or at least the queen's dreams – not a mistake by a forgetful apprentice."

The young fairy gulped and looked down, trying to force back tears of regret.

"I'm sorry that I messed things up. From now on, I'll only do as you say."

"You'd better. Rashly granted wishes can contain mistakes and those can ruin the path of destiny for anyone who is affected by those flaws. We can only hope that this one here will turn out just fine."

𝔑𝔦𝔫𝔢 months later, the queen gave birth to her first child. It was a long night and the belly of the queen had become so big that the king was sure it had to be a strong and sturdy prince who would be born.

All the more he was surprised to hear the voice of the midwife as the groaning of the queen subsided.

"It's a girl!"

And it was indeed. The moment that the queen and king laid eyes on her, they fell deeply in love with their child. There was already a curl of black hair on her tiny head and the queen smiled when she looked into the pale face with red cheeks.

"Skin as white as snow, lips as red as blood and hair as black as ebony wood – you shall be named Snow White and will surely be the fairest of all princesses ever born."

"Snow White it shall be," agreed the king and looked upon the baby with fond eyes. "She already is the prettiest girl I've ever seen – next to you, my queen."

Queen and king smiled down on their cute small baby. Little Snow White was hungry though and quickly demanded to be fed. The queen snuggled her up against her bosom and let her drink the warm mother's milk, while she hummed a joyful tune.

But just as little Snow White had finished, the queen flinched and put her hand upon her belly, which was still round as a water melon.

"I think," she groaned, "there is a second one coming."

The eyes of the king widened as the midwife hurried towards them and put her hands on the queen's belly.

"Good Heavens! She's right. There is a twin on its way!"

In a rush, little Snow White was taken away from her mother's breast and laid into the father's arm instead. He looked down into the tiny face and was lost in its beauty, while the queen was in labour once more. This time, it took a bit longer than before and the queen groaned and breathed hard, but then it was over and her second daughter was born.

"Another girl," the midwife stated as she put the tiny creature into her mother's arms. "I sure hope that this was the last one or else I'll be up all night!"

The midwife's wish was granted as there were no more babies to be born this night. While the king was still gazing happily at Snow White, the queen looked down upon her second child in wonder.

"I didn't even ask for two children. But here they are. Two beautiful girls, so small and fragile."

Her eyes took in the curl of red hair on the second child's head and she arched her brows. *I just hope that this is not a bad omen …*

Just when the king walked over towards his wife to see his second-born child, the tiny creature opened her eyes for the split of a second.

"Good Lord!" the king exclaimed and stepped back, putting a protective arm around Snow White. "Those eyes! They are black like the darkest night –"

"No," whispered the queen. "Black like ebony wood."

And she smiled down on the child that had once again closed its eyes and was drinking the warm mother's milk with hungry gulps.

"Black like ebony wood?" repeated the king and looked from the queen to Snow White and back again. "Well, I definitely like the black *hair* better. But if those eyes stay as black as they are now, it would be fitting to call her Ebony."

"Ebony," mumbled the queen. "Yes, I like that."

And she pressed little Ebony to her bosom, just above her heart and started to hum a cheerful melody, while the little princess was drinking the warm mother's milk, looking happy but pale.

"There's no colour in those cheeks," murmured the midwife with worry in her eyes. "I can only hope that she's sturdy enough to survive the coming winter."

"She'll be fine," said the queen with a tired but merry face. "Her skin is as white as the snow. I'm sure that's a sign that she and winter were made for each other."

The queen should be proven right.

While little Snow White was a bit feeble in the beginning and didn't seem to like the cold very much, little Ebony flourished and grew, even when the snow started to fall early at the very beginning of winter. As the queen stood with her on one of the balconies, a snowflake found its way onto the pale cheek of the tiny princess, which lay in the arms of her mother, gazing up at the starry sky.

When the snowflake touched her skin, little Ebony smiled and giggled and the queen couldn't help but return the joyful smile.

"You are strong, my love," she whispered to Ebony, who had closed her eyes and listened to the beating heart of her mother. "You will survive this winter and all the ones to come, I'm sure of that – no matter how pale your skin might seem. It was I who wished for that, so I'm sure it will prove to be a strength, not a weakness."

And once again, the queen was right. Against the worries of the midwife, Ebony was a strong and sturdy child, small but unharmed by the cold.

Snow White on the other hand seemed to love the warmth of summer much better and started to thrive as soon as the days lengthened and the sun warmed her pretty little face. She soon grew to be a cute and beautiful little girl, always loved and protected by her parents.

Especially her father loved her the most. Being taken aback by the black eyes of his second daughter, he mostly spent time with Snow White, while the queen loved them both and treated them equally.

Little Ebony though, feeling the reserve of her father, clung to her mother and started to cry whenever the midwife or one of the servant girls tried to take her away. It took a couple of months until Ebony finally quieted down a bit and would at least part from her mother for a few hours a day.

But even when Ebony learned how to walk – being quicker than Snow White, who was carried around by her father very often – she mostly followed her mother and didn't want to leave her side, unless she was playing with her sister.

All the while, little Ebony was faster at learning new things than Snow White. She was more curious and would try out new things without fear of failure.

The servants called her 'nosy little Ebony', because she would always crawl into the tiniest corners, being curious to investigate which secrets might be hidden in the dark. Her curiosity seemed to be growing even faster than her body and was often encouraged by the queen.

"Snow White might be the fairest," she once told Ebony, while the little princess was sitting on her lap, "but you will be wiser than her, because you always seek the truth and get to the bottom of things."

Ebony looked up to her mother with round eyes, trying to wrap her mind around the word 'wisdom'. It took a few years until she truly understood what the queen had said to her that day, but all the while she was sure that it had to be something important.

At the very same time, Snow White was sitting on her father's lap in the throne room, gazing up at him with warm brown eyes.

"You have the eyes of your mother," the king told her with a fond smile, "and her beauty too. You will be the most wonderful princess the world has ever known. And if my wife shouldn't bear me a son, you will be the queen of this land one day. The whole thing about an only male heritage line is nonsense anyway!"

The king made sure to stick to his word and when it seemed like his wife wouldn't bear any children to him within the next years, he established a law which allowed the female heirs of a king to take over the throne in the cause of the king's death.

Snow White and Ebony grew up to be kind at heart and loved by everyone. While the eldest was adored for her beauty and charm, Ebony was liked for her sharp mind and words of advice. She was clever from an early age and always spoke true-heartedly, never trying to conceal it if she had done anything wrong.

"There is something strange about her though," some of the servants rumoured amongst each other. "Her eyes are as black as the night. And her hair looks like it was drenched in blood."

They never said those things out loud in front of the royal family and always acted friendly towards Ebony. But deep in their hearts they were a little afraid of the younger princess.

And they were not altogether wrong. There was something mysterious and peculiar about Ebony from time to time.

While Snow White danced through the sunshine and let butterflies sit on her fingers, little Ebony was crawling in the dirt, watching beetles, worms and ants.

"Isn't it amazing how much weight they can carry?" she once said to Snow White while studying a line of ants which were carrying huge burdens upon their backs.

Snow White didn't even bother to take her gaze away from the clouds she was looking at and just kept smiling happily, while she replied: "I'd rather be a bird – light and free, flying through the air as if nothing could stop me."

Ebony looked up and eyed her big sister with a frown.

"What kind of bird would you like to be?" she inquired, trying to understand Snow White's desire. "And where would you fly to?"

"I don't know," answered Snow White with a dreamy look on her face. "I'd just fly around, I guess. Looking down onto the world. Maybe I could be a swallow –"

"Why not a magpie?" mocked Ebony. "They are black and white, just like you are."

"I'm not just black and white!"

"Of course, you are. Black hair, white skin – apart from those ridiculously red cheeks and lips, you're very much like a magpie, I think."

"I don't want to be a magpie! They steal things."

"Nonsense. Only sometimes they take glittery things which they like – pretty much the same as you. Whenever father gives you a shiny new necklace, your eyes sparkle like the diamonds around your neck."

"I'm not like a magpie!" Snow White said outraged. "I'd rather be a swallow or a singing bird."

"Whatever you want, sis," Ebony replied with a shrug. "Anyway, it sure would be interesting to see the castle from above." She lay down in the grass to watch the clouds and birds pass by. "I'd be a falcon, small and fast, so that no one could catch me."

"Who would want to catch you?"

"I don't know. Predator birds maybe. Or humans. But I'd be too fast for them. I would fly into the woods and watch the other animals. Or I'd visit the villages in our kingdom and see how the people live."

Snow White gave her little sister a puzzled look. She had never thought much about the circumstances of the people in the realm.

"Don't you think they live just like we do?" she asked Ebony while she returned her gaze towards the sky, looking for funny shapes in the clouds.

"Of course not. We live in a castle – they live in small houses of brick or wood. It must be very different from our way of living. They don't have a cook and still have to provide food for their children. They work in the fields or as a blacksmith or carpenter. It must be fascinating to watch them … or maybe even join them and learn how to work like they do."

"Now you've lost it," said Snow White and laughed her cute bell-like laughter. "You are a princess! We don't work among the common folk. And we surely don't perform tiring tasks like working in the fields, getting all dirty and ruining our soft skin."

Ebony looked down upon her fingers, which were covered in dirt, because she had been digging up the earth, searching for animals she might not know yet.

"Why would dirt be a problem? You can wash it off as soon as you have finished your work."

"A princess shouldn't get dirty in the first place," sighed Snow White, wishing that Ebony would just shut up and let her gaze at the clouds in peace.

"In that case," Ebony concluded, "being a princess is one of the most boring things in the world! I'd rather be an ant, crawling around on the ground and being able to carry things which weigh several times as much as I do."

Snow White didn't reply to that and Ebony understood the silent hint. She was used to dealing with her thoughts of curiosity on her own and turned to watch a raven which was sitting in one of the trees within the castle garden. *He has got black eyes, just like mine. But he is free to leave and fly wherever he wants to go, not being bound by a human body or human laws. Maybe Snow White is right. Being a bird would be quite interesting!*

At the same time as Snow White and Ebony were watching the clouds in the sky, the Good Fairy and her apprentice were sitting in the Cloud Castle amongst those very same clouds, gazing into one of the mirrors which showed the two princesses from above.

"Snow White is turning into a real beauty," stated the Good Fairy with a cheerful voice. She was proud of her work and satisfied with the child she had bestowed upon the queen.

"Ebony is pretty as well," Arabella mumbled and eyed the pale princess with pride. "And she is witty. I like that."

"You might like it. But you are too idealistic for this age. Men of this time prefer good-looking women who are obedient and don't make trouble."

"Isn't that discriminating?"

"It is. But there is nothing we can do about it."

"But that's unfair," moaned the young fairy. "Why can't we just put a spell on the men and make them more open-minded towards intelligent women?"

"That would be a violation of our Fairy Code! We only use our magic to grant wishes – not to manipulate the world as we see fit. It's not in our hands what is meant to be or not. The humans have to learn about equal rights by themselves."

"Shouldn't we try to help them?"

"No," the Good Fairy exclaimed emphatically. "That's not our task. You should be satisfied that Snow White's beauty got the king to establish a new law for the female line of heritage. Now a princess can become a queen without being married to a king. Snow White might as well be the next queen of this land after the king's death."

"Humph," grumbled the young fairy and folded her arms, while she watched the two princesses lying on the grass. *Ebony would make a better queen. She's smart and righteous, while Snow White mostly cares about her dresses and other pretty things in life. She is way too naive to be a queen …*

When Snow White and Ebony were about six years old, the queen got very ill. She grew paler from day to day and at some point, she was so weak that she wasn't able to leave her bed anymore.

The king was very worried and sent for the wisest men in the whole kingdom, but none of them were able to help the queen to overcome her sickness.

Snow White brought flowers to the queen's bedside every day and sang to the queen, filling the chamber with her pure, high voice.

"You'll be better soon, mother, right?" Snow White asked, every time that she had finished her song and was about to go back outside and play in the sun.

"Of course, my darling," the queen replied with a feeble voice and tried to smile. "You already made me feel much better, my little sunshine."

Snow White would always return the smile, give her mother a hug and then run into the garden to forget her sorrow and watch the clouds instead.

Ebony on the other hand could not forget her worries. She sometimes stayed at the bedside of her mother for hours when the king wasn't there, just caressing her hand and telling her about what she had discovered that day.

One time, she even brought a book of fairy tales to the queen. When her mother saw it, she sighed and shook her head with a sad look.

"I can't read to you, Ebony. My voice won't last –"

"I know, mother. But I can read *to you*. It always made me feel better when you read those stories to me while I was young and couldn't sleep."

"You're still young, my child –"

"Yes, but not *that* young anymore!"

"Go ahead then," whispered the queen with a fragile smile upon her pale lips. "Read to me."

And Ebony read to her stories of adventures, of princes and princesses, of dragons and fairies and lots of other things that she loved.

The queen listened, smiled and sometimes even laughed, enjoying the distraction from her aching body. Ebony had a way of storytelling that made all the tales feel very much alive whenever she lent them her voice.

"Thank you very much, my dear," breathed the queen when Ebony had finished yet another story. "I already feel much more alive again."

"Will you ever get better though?" asked Ebony with a look of earnest worry on her face.

"I don't know," answered the queen reluctantly. "I'm afraid not. None of the wise men your father gathered here was able to help me."

"What about wise women? Aren't there herb-wives who could cure you?"

"Your father doesn't believe in herbalism. He is afraid that those herb women might be witches."

"That's nonsense," Ebony mumbled irritated, but tried not to upset her mother with her own feelings. "Well … Can I help you?"

"Oh, my sweet little Ebony! You've already done so much for me. Those hours we spent in the lands of fairies and dragons have been the most beautiful ones since I've been tied to my bed."

"But there's got to be a way to heal you from your sickness," insisted Ebony desperately. "Or at least to ease your pain. You shouldn't have to die in agony!"

The queen flinched. She had always tried to hide it whenever she was in pain and even though she was much more open with Ebony than she was with Snow White, she never had guessed that Ebony would find out how close she was to death.

"We don't know yet if I'm going to die," she tried to comfort her daughter. "Maybe I'll get better now that you've reminded me of how wonderful and adventurous life can be. Don't lose hope, darling."

"I'll never lose hope! But it's obvious that you have been getting worse every single day. How can I still believe that you'll get better at some point?"

Ebony's eyes started to get wet, like the dark but shiny surface of a lake at night. The queen looked at her with despair and couldn't help but admire the strange beauty of her daughter's looks.

"Whatever people say to you," she whispered, "you are beautiful and wonderful and the most loveable daughter a mother could wish for. To some, your eyes might look like a blank night sky, but to me, there's more. I can see stars sparkling upon that black sky, shining with curiosity and wisdom, to enlighten the world and the minds of the people around you."

"The people won't listen to a weird redhead like me."

"Of course, they will! They'll have to! Don't ever believe that your looks make you less worthy. Never lose hope, darling. I have faith in you. And if *you* believe in yourself, too, you can accomplish anything you want. You choose your own destiny. Never forget that."

And with those words, the queen passed away, a loving smile upon her face, leaving behind two grieving daughters and a heartbroken king, who secretly blamed Ebony for the death of his wife.

"You shouldn't have read so many stories to her at once," he chided his youngest daughter soon after the funeral. "It was too tiring for her!"

"But she liked it," Ebony replied in her defence. "She smiled and laughed and didn't tell me to stop. She even said that these were the most joyful moments she'd had in weeks!"

"When did you learn to read anyway? Even Snow White can't read yet –"

"Even?? I'm always faster than her, in case you haven't noticed," Ebony retorted defiantly. "She doesn't even give it a try! She preferred it when mother read the stories to her and not even looked at the letters and words in the book. How could she ever learn to read them?"

"Don't talk bad of your sister!" the king rebuked her. "Anyway … It was too much for the queen! Reading to her for hours and hours … You should have known better."

"But she wanted me to read on!"

"You should have given her a break though. Given her some time to rest in between, to gather new strength –"

"I didn't kill her," shouted Ebony, starting to sob. "It wasn't my fault that she died. She said herself that she wasn't feeling any better."

"But she could have! She would have felt better someday, I'm sure! We would have found a way to –"

"– heal her? No. There was no way. She said so herself. I tried to find one, but there was nothing to be done. There was no cure for her sickness. At least not while you wouldn't let in the herb-wives –"

"Don't dare to speak of those silly witches!" yelled the king and lifted his hand as if to slap his daughter.

Ebony flinched, but didn't try to get out of the way. She looked at her father with angry determination, not afraid to meet whatever punishment he thought necessary.

The king stopped dead in midair, meeting the gaze of those deep black eyes he secretly feared, but which showed no fear themselves. With a heavy sigh he lowered his hand.

"I'm sorry for yelling at you. It wasn't your fault that she died, I know that. I just miss her so much!"

"So do I," mumbled Ebony and started to weep openly.

The king stepped forward to embrace her in his strong arms, but Ebony's pale skin reminded him of the dead face of his wife and rooted him to the spot.

Ebony, left alone with her sorrow, turned on her heels and ran down into the cellar, where she could be alone and hide from the cruel world which rejected her. *Now that my mother is gone, who is left to love me?*

$\mathfrak{Like}$ any man who had lost the love of his life, the king moaned for the queen for a long time. He only found comfort in Snow White's brown eyes, which reminded him of that of her mother, and in her joyful insouciance, which quickly returned and filled the castle with laughter once more.

Snow White had loved her mother dearly, but she wasn't hurt by her loss just as much as her father or sister. She was more carefree and soon saw the bright side of life again, while the rest of the castle still grieved over the death of their beloved queen.

Soon enough, Snow White danced through the garden, remembering her mother's joyful face whenever she looked upon the flowers, whereas Ebony hid in the darkest places of the castle, filled by sorrow and loneliness.

Death had taken away the only person who ever truly loved and understood her, leaving her with nothing but memories and dreams, which seemed to grow paler every day that the queen was not around.

The king didn't exactly mind Ebony's absence. He had no idea how to comfort her anyway and was rather relieved whenever Ebony occasionally skipped one of the meals, being too filled with grief to even think of eating.

Snow White, on the other hand, often tried to cheer up her younger sister and sang joyful tunes all day long or brought food to her chamber, but to no effect.

Ebony became thinner and even more pale than she had been before, looking more like a ghost than ever. Her dark red hair stood out against the whiteness of her skin and gave the servants a chill whenever they found her, lurking in the darkness of the cellar.

One whole year passed in that manner, until the king finally decided to marry again. The new queen was a beautiful and proud woman, the likes of which had never been seen in the castle before.

While the former queen had been very pretty, kind, loving and charming, there was something cold about the beauty of the new queen. Her face was like a mask and she seldomly smiled, as if she was missing a sense of humour.

"Why would father marry someone as earnest and icy as her?" whispered Ebony to Snow White when they first laid eyes on the bride of the king during the wedding ceremony.

"I think she's beautiful," answered Snow White in a low voice and admired the pure and soft skin of the new queen.

"I don't like her looks," countered Ebony with a frown. "There is something cagey about her. As if she is hiding a part of herself – maybe even a dark secret."

"Oh, come on," sighed Snow White. "There is absolutely nothing dark about her!"

"Not in her looks maybe," mumbled Ebony and eyed the bride in white with a feeling of mistrust.

Snow White was right though: On the outside, there was nothing dark about the new queen. Her eyes were a light shade of blue, like a cloudless summer sky and her hair was light blonde, almost white, like a veil of liquid stars, framing her fair face.

"She's nearly as pale as you are," mocked Snow White.

"I'm nothing like her," Ebony insisted. "There is something wicked about her. Even her beauty seems false. Like a mask behind which she's hiding her true self."

"Nonsense! Her beauty is breathtaking! No wonder that father wants to marry her. Who could withstand such a flawless face? Admit it, Ebony: You're just jealous that she's more beautiful than you are."

"I'm not jealous!"

Ebony crossed her arms and watched the bride walking through the high halls of the church towards their father. The king only had eyes for the radiant beauty and Ebony couldn't help but feel an urge to protect him. *He is blinded by her looks. But has he ever dared to look within? Does he know if she's as pure at heart as her skin is flawless?*

"She is definitely not my type," Ebony grumbled, causing Snow White to turn to her with wide eyes.

"Of course, she's not. You are a woman and so is she. Or," she added with a teasing voice, "are you suddenly into women now?"

"Maybe," Ebony shrugged. "I'm more into the character of a person than their sex. Man or woman – does that really matter?"

"I guess not. But I'd still prefer a strong and handsome prince over any woman!"

"Well, I would prefer *anyone* over *her*," Ebony concluded, turning her attention back to the new queen.

There was nothing she could do to prevent the marriage though and so she just stood and watched, hoping that her instincts were wrong. And at first it seemed as if her gut feeling might have been mistaken indeed.

The new queen didn't smile, but she was nice enough to be likeable and put everyone under her charm with her dazzling beauty. The male servants all lost their hearts to her, while the female servants tried to imitate her elaborate hairstyle and admired her pretty dresses.

Ebony still didn't like to be around her and secretly named her 'Ice Queen', because she was always so cold and earnest. Otherwise there seemed to be nothing wrong about her and Ebony tried her best to be the polite princess whenever she encountered the new queen – which did not happen all too often.

The Ice Queen would not go into the cellar or any dark place of the castle. She preferred the light-filled halls and the garden and demanded that the whole south tower was made hers so that her chambers would be filled by the warming rays of the sun.

As soon as the king had granted that wish, nobody was allowed to enter the south tower anymore and even the servants only went into the main chamber of the queen, never going up to the top floor again.

"But the south tower has the best view," Snow White exclaimed as the king told them about this. "Why can't we go up there anymore? We wouldn't disturb the new queen, I promise."

"I'm sorry, my sweetheart," replied the king with apologising eyes. "But she won't have anyone up there. I think we should just respect her privacy. The west tower does have a nice view as well, especially at sunrise."

"True," Snow White agreed and thus the matter was solved for her.

Ebony on the other hand didn't understand why the new queen would want a whole tower for herself and asked her father about it when she found him all alone in the throne room one evening.

"Father?"

The king gave a start and turned towards her with surprise on his face, but then tried to relax and look kindly upon his young daughter.

"Yes, my dear?"

"Why would one person need a whole tower for herself? Don't you think that this is strange?"

"No."

"Really? But not even the servants are allowed up there! How does she keep the place clean? Does she do it herself?"

"I don't know, my dear. She didn't tell me and I won't ask. It's just the way it is now."

"But why?" Ebony dug deeper. "What is she doing up there? Does she need all the chambers for her endless flow of gorgeous dresses and jewellery?"

"I really don't know. I haven't been up there myself ever since she claimed it for herself."

"Seriously? Not even *you* are allowed up there?"

"Of course, I'd be allowed," the king laughed surprised. "I'm the king and this is my castle. But I don't see the necessity to go there. Why would I? There is nothing bad about a little privacy."

"But what if she's hiding something?"

"That's enough now, Ebony!"

The king got up from his throne and looked at his child with stern eyes and a frown.

"But father –"

"No! I don't want to hear about this ever again. Do you understand me?"

"Yes, your highness."

Ebony quickly left the throne room and fled to her own chambers, holding back tears of frustration and anger. *Why does nobody else think of this as suspicious? Am I the only one who is not falling for this ethereal beauty?*

for a few weeks, Ebony tried to hold back her suspicion. She did her best to act normal, attending all meals and not speaking up, unless she was asked to say something.

But one morning, while the king and queen were gone for a coach ride, Ebony couldn't resist the urge to sneak up to the south tower. She waited until none of the servants were around and slipped silently into the main chamber of the new queen.

It was a large bedroom, with high glassed windows and a picturesque view of the landscape. There was nothing out of the ordinary – at least if you called gilded mirrors and dressers normal – and thus, Ebony ventured on towards the staircase, which led up to the other chambers of the tower.

On the first landing, there was a dressing room, filled with the most exquisite dresses and jewellery that Ebony had ever seen. In every corner, there seemed to be something sparkly or shiny and she was sure that Snow White would have had a hard time keeping away from all those glittery things. *Good thing that she is the magpie from the two of us!*

Ebony turned her back on the dressing room and went up another landing, where she found a room filled with herbs and weird looking plants. The scent of dried herbs and flowers hung in the air like a very strong perfume. *Amazing enough that the Ice Queen doesn't smell of herbs. There is more of a flowery fragrance about her – but maybe that's just a way to cover the scent.*

After a quick look around, Ebony carefully closed the door to the herbs chamber again and went up to the top floor of the tower. When she reached the door, she found that it was locked though. Frustration welled up inside her, while she examined the keyhole with a scrutinising look. *This is not an ordinary lock. It looks different than the others in the castle. Did the queen install it there herself? But what could she be hiding inside?!*

There was no way to satisfy her curiosity as there was no key to be seen. Ebony rushed down into the main chamber once more and searched the bed and dressers, but without success. There was no key and thus no way to unveil the secrets of the locked chamber. *I'll find a way one day! There's got to be a way to open that door.*

Ebony hurriedly left the south tower and went back to her own chamber, to ponder on a possibility to open the strange lock.

At first, she thought of using hairpins, but quickly cast away that idea, because the thin pins wouldn't even work on the ordinary lock in her own room.

Her second thought was to use knitting needles, but those were not flexible enough to deal with the elaborate windings of the keyhole to the secret chamber.

In the end, she had to give up on her task of solving this mystery altogether, because winter came and the new queen wouldn't leave the castle anymore as soon as the first frost had arrived.

It was way too dangerous to try to sneak up into the south tower while the Ice Queen was around and Ebony tried to keep her mind busy with other things instead. As soon as the first snow fell, she spent most of her time outside, watching the snowflakes glide down from the sky and settling upon her cold palm.

She admired the silent dance of the icy crystals, while they glided down from heaven, and realised that they were far more fascinating than the new queen. *Maybe Ice Queen isn't such a fitting name for her anyway. She doesn't like winter, she won't go out into the cold and she'd never allow her perfect hairstyle to be 'ruined' by the snow.*

As Snow White preferred the protective warmth of the castle, too, Ebony was spending the days of winter mostly on her own. Even the servants would only come out into the garden to tell her that she should not stay outside for too long.

"You'll catch a cold," warned one of the nursemaids when she escorted Ebony back inside to make her ready for dinner. "A princess shouldn't stay out in the snow. You'll get your dress all wet. And your feet must be icy!"

"As a matter of fact, my feet are fine and so am I," Ebony replied irritated. "I don't mind the cold. And my boots are thick enough to keep my feet warm."

"But your hands! Your fingers are cold as ice."

"Well, they are as pale as snow too. Seems fitting for them to be cold, doesn't it?"

To that, the maiden didn't say anything, because she was afraid that she might let slip that she found Ebony's looks weird and scary.

At the dinner table, Ebony stayed all silent and watched the fair queen from the corner of her eyes, until the king suddenly put down his knife and fork and looked around him with a beam.

"Who wants to go for a sleigh ride tomorrow? It's supposed to be a nice day without much wind and a beautiful view over the snowy landscape."

"No, no," the queen answered immediately. "It's far too cold for me. I couldn't stand it to be out there for such a long time."

"We can take pelts and blankets with us," the king tried to persuade his new wife, but in vain.

"I couldn't! I'd catch a cold and die. I'm not made for winter. I was born in summer and I prefer the warmth of the hearth for now."

The king sighed and looked towards Snow White.

"What about you, my dearest?"

"Oh, no, father. I don't really like the cold either."

She smiled at the queen, who lifted the corner of her mouth for a second as if to smile in return. Her eyes stayed cold and untouched though.

"But the land looks beautiful," the king raved. "Maybe the sun will be out. It's supposed to be a clear day tomorrow. The snow will sparkle like thousand diamonds. Wouldn't you like that?"

"I don't know, father. I really wouldn't want to catch a cold. I prefer the summer as well. And I can watch the snow sparkle through the windows."

She and the new queen fit together perfectly, Ebony thought to herself, while she rolled her eyes and looked down upon her food. *They have a lot in common: They both hate the cold and are used to being the most beautiful beings in the room – even though Snow White is not as icy as the queen. The only question is: Who will be more beautiful when Snow White finally grows up …?*

"Well, I guess, we'll just stay inside," said the king with a heavy sigh. "Too bad. It's really supposed to be a very fine day tomorrow –"

"I'd like to go," Ebony said quickly, looking up from her plate. "I'd love to go for a sleigh ride and see the snowy landscape. I love the snow!"

She tried to smile, while she gazed up at her father with hidden hope, her heart beating fast. He looked back with a puzzled look on his face, staying silent for a few seconds.

"I see," he finally managed to say. "It'll be the two of us then … Or would any of the other ladies like to accompany us, now that we've decided to go anyway?"

Both the queen and Snow White shook their heads with furious determination. The king sighed once more and tried to smile at Ebony.

"The two of us it shall be. I'll tell the stable master to prepare the sleigh for us soon after midday. The sun should be out by then and we'll have a glorious view over the landscape."

He darted a glance at Snow White, who didn't seem to be interested in the matter at all. *I'm really going to spend some time with my father all on my own! And he won't be able to escape from any of my questions. That'll be my chance to find out whether he knows anything suspicious about his new wife.*

𝕿𝖍𝖊 following day held its promises. The sun went up as soon as the moon and stars had cleared the sky and enlightened the newly fallen snow, which covered the landscape with a thick blanket of sparkly white.

"Isn't it beautiful?" the king exclaimed during breakfast and started another try to convince his new wife or Snow White to come along for the sleigh ride.

Both of them refused to leave the castle though and thus the king was left with no other choice, but to take Ebony for a ride instead. They went out into the castle courtyard shortly after midday and covered themselves with pelts as soon as they had sat down in the open sleigh.

"You're right, father," Ebony agreed when they had left the castle behind and were driving through the snowy landscape of hills. "It is very beautiful!"

The king smiled and nodded, while he, too, watched the sparkling fields and trees pass by beside them. They enjoyed the beauty of the land in silence for a while, until Ebony decided that it was time to use her chance and ask her father about the secretive behaviour of the new queen.

Just as she opened her mouth though, the king sighed happily and turned towards her with a relieved smile.

"I'm glad that you and my new wife seem to get along now," he said and winked at her. "I was really worried that you might make trouble about the whole affair with the south tower. But it seems I misjudged you. I was too harsh on you and I'm sorry."

Ebony stared at her father, her mouth half open and felt her determination freeze, as if the snow had entered her brain and turned her resolve to ice.

"Maybe I should have introduced you to her earlier," the king went on, now lost in thoughts and gazing into the distance. "Before the wedding. But it all happened so quickly. I was deeply in love – and still am."

Sure! Blinded by her beauty would be more accurate. Ebony bit back her dislike for the new queen and tried to see her with the eyes of her father. *Does he really love her?*

"I hope that you two will get along from now on," the king finished his monologue and looked down at Ebony once more. "I can understand if you miss your mother. I miss her too! But she won't come back and we have to move on – as a family."

Ebony gulped. The questions about the secret chamber burned on her tongue, but she couldn't bring herself to ask them, facing her father's happy face.

"I shall try my best," she replied instead and returned the smile, feeling her heart melt and picking up its pace. *Could it be that father is actually starting to love ME as well? Has he finally accepted me as his daughter?*

"I'm sure you'll do great, my dear," the king encouraged her hopes with a fond smile. "We'll just all do our best and get through this together. As a family. A happy family."

That would be wonderful!

Warm joy streamed through Ebony's whole body and she leaned against her father's arm, a smile spreading over her face which rivalled with the shiny glow of the snow around them.

$\mathcal{A}\mathfrak{s}$ time passed, Ebony and her father grew a little closer every day. He never loved her as dearly as Snow White, but that didn't matter to her. She was happy that he was spending some time with her once in a while. And happiness was very becoming to her.

Soon after the sleigh ride with her father, she started to eat normally again and gained some weight, much to the delight of the servants, because it made her look less like a ghost.

She didn't lurk around in the cellar anymore, too, and often enjoyed the sunny days of winter playing in the snowy gardens of the castle.

It was only then that the king actually noticed how pretty Ebony was, even though her looks were nothing compared to the beauty of Snow White, which seemed to be growing with every new summer that she experienced.

The new queen gave not much thought to the changes that both Ebony and Snow White were going through. She didn't like children and mostly ignored them, preferring to spend her time alone with the king.

He on the other hand was growing fonder of his two daughters every day and boasted about the beauty of Snow White when he visited the neighboring kingdoms.

Whenever he left the castle, he put the queen in charge of everything, trusting her blindly and never doubting that she would act as kindly and just as he did.

As children, neither Snow White nor Ebony had paid much attention to the duties of their father and didn't bother to think how one might reign a kingdom.

When they had grown up a bit though and turned thirteen just before a very icy winter, Ebony started to visit her father when he was dealing with the requests and concerns of the people. She listened to his wise words and fair judgement and tried to understand how he decided what was wrong and what was right.

"How do you know that nobody's lying to you?" she once asked him after listening to hours of complaints, wishes and miseries of the people.

"If someone is lying, they won't be able to look me in the eye for a long time," the king explained wisely. "To the people I'm something close to a god. They look up to me and wouldn't dare to lie to me, because they know that my judgement is fair."

"But if someone *was* lying to you? How would you know what's true and what's a lie?"

"Lies can't live forever – the truth can. If you think that something is a lie, you only have to look closer and closer, until it reveals its true self. If a person would be lying to *you*, for example, you could just keep questioning them about the details of their statement. If it's a lie, there will be flaws and they might even confuse parts of their story, until they are entangled in their own lies."

"And truth lives forever?"

"Yes. Truth does never fade nor stumble. It is like an eternal flame, enlightening our lives and shining within the eyes of those who are wise and truthful at heart."

Ebony was very impressed by this. From that day on, she always tried to sense whether someone was lying to her or not, practising her skills while she watched her father during the fulfilment of his kingly duties.

As soon as she thought that she knew how to tell truth and lies apart, she kept close watch on the queen for a few weeks, trying to find out whether she was a deceiving liar.

It was hard to judge the queen though, because she didn't spend much time with the children. Ebony mostly saw her during meals, but she did her best to pay close attention to what the king and queen were talking about and whether the queen seemed to be honest with him.

There was definitely no sparkle of truth to be seen in the cold eyes of the queen – only self-love, arrogance and pride. *There is a coldness even to her beauty*, Ebony thought to herself, *very unlike the beauty of Snow White. My sister is all warm and kind, radiating with joy and happiness. It won't take long until she will surpass the icy mask of beauty on the queen's face.*

Soon enough, spring came and with it the blooming power of life, growth and youth. Snow White was by far the fairest sight in the castle garden, even though the latter was filled with flowers of all colours and scents, between which Snow White loved to play in the warming sun.

Even the queen couldn't deny the blooming beauty of Snow White anymore and Ebony noticed that the queen was eyeing the princess with loathing looks from time to time.

But neither the king nor Snow White seemed to notice this and Ebony didn't dare to mention it, not wanting to destroy the fragile bond which finally connected her and her father.

One day, when the king rode off again to visit one of the neighbouring kingdoms and left the queen in charge of everything at the castle, Ebony decided to follow her and find out what she was doing all day long while her husband was away.

This wasn't an easy task, because the queen was very secretive and often vanished into her chambers in the south tower. Ebony watched the queen within the throne room though, where Ebony hid behind one of the stone statues and listened to the pleas and matters of the people, who had come to seek the king's help.

In contrast to the king, the queen wasn't very kind with her judgement. She treated the peasants like scum, eyeing them with cold disgust and often enough sending them home with tears in their eyes. *She is neither fair nor just! I have to tell father about this when he gets back.*

When the queen had dealt with the concerns of the people, she went back into her own chambers, telling her servants that she didn't want to be disturbed.

Ebony silently followed her and peeked through the keyhole into the bedroom of the queen. There wasn't much to be seen, but when she strained her ears, she could sometimes hear the queen mutter to herself.

After a while, everything went silent within the chamber and Ebony wasn't able to see the silhouette of the queen anymore. She waited for a few seconds, until she was sure that there was no movement within. Then she pushed down the doorhandle and peeked through the crack of the door. There was no one inside. *She must have gone up into one of the other chambers – maybe even the secret chamber! This is my chance.*

Quickly, but careful not to make a sound, Ebony slipped into the room and closed the door behind her. On tiptoes she went towards the stone staircase and climbed up to the first landing.

A glance through the keyhole told her that the queen wasn't inside and she ventured on as quietly as possible.

When she reached the next landing, she held her breath and peeked into the herbs chamber. It was rather dark and gloomy, because the only window was being blocked by all the dried plants. Ebony narrowed her eyes and tried to make out whether there was any movement within the chamber. There was no one to be seen though and she stepped back with a silent sigh. *That means that the secret chamber is open right now!*

Her heart started to race. Excitement quickened her pace, though she tried her best not to make a sound. When she reached the top of the tower, the door to the secret chamber was unlocked and stood ajar a little, proving that the queen had to be inside.

Ebony held her breath once more as she approached the wooden door and tried to peek through the small crack into the secret chamber. *There she is!*

And she was indeed. The queen stood tall and proud in front of a gilded mirror, which was hanging on one of the side walls. From where she stood, Ebony wasn't able to see the queen's reflection, but it seemed like she was actually looking at something – or someone – else, to whom she was speaking in a commanding voice.

"Mirror, mirror, on the wall, who is the fairest of us all?"

Ebony furrowed her brow, not sure whether she had misheard anything. *Is she seriously talking to herself in the mirror?*

Her silent question was answered within seconds, as a voice, very unlike the one of the queen, spoke next. It seemed to be coming out of nowhere, but then Ebony realised that it actually had to be the voice of the mirror. *A magic mirror! She's got to be a witch!*

"The fairest one is you, my queen. The fairest that has ever been."

"And ever shall be," added the queen smugly. "This little Snow White might be pretty, but even she can't rival my beauty!"

Not yet, thought Ebony with worry. *But if she keeps growing more beautiful during the summer, it won't take long until she surpasses the beauty of the queen. What will happen then? Will the queen talk father into marrying her off to some prince far, far away?*

Ebony didn't dare to think about what else the queen might do to ensure that she was the most beautiful woman within the kingdom. *I just hope she won't hurt Snow White. I could never let that happen!*

𝕎𝕙𝕖𝕟 the king got back from his journey, Ebony instantly tried to talk to him. The queen kept him all to herself though, lulling him with words of love and longing. *As if she truly missed him. Ha! She seemed rather happy to have the castle all to herself while he was gone. I'm sure she only wants him to tell her how beautiful she is all day long.*

For a few days, Ebony tried in vain to get a chance to see her father alone. The queen even accompanied him into the throne room, attending the hearings of the peasants and people of the realm. *Maybe she wants to make sure that they won't complain about her. But I will – as soon as I get the chance.*

To Ebony's frustration, the queen didn't seem to want to give her a chance to speak to her father alone. *Is she suspecting something?*

Ebony didn't know if the queen was actually able to use her magic mirror to spy on other people and thus couldn't be sure if she'd ever be able to talk to her father in private again. She didn't give up on trying though.

After a couple of days of fruitless efforts, she decided to take matters into her own hands and get rid of the queen by herself – at least for a few minutes. She sneaked into the kitchen and nicked a bit of beetroot, which she put onto the queen's chair in the dining room.

When everybody was getting seated for lunch, Ebony watched the queen from the corner of her eyes, while she was pretending to be in conversation with Snow White, who was happily chattering about the flowers which she had picked for her room.

"Ugh!"

The high-pitched scream of the queen made them all jump. Ebony, too, tried to look as surprised as possible, while she looked towards the queen. Everyone turned to her and several servants rushed over to see what was wrong.

"What in the name of –?!" the queen ranted on, until she spotted the beetroot on her chair. "What is this? Who of you stupid, ignorant numbskulls let food fall onto my chair?! You have ruined the back of my dress!!"

Icy spears of fury seemed to be emitting from her light blue eyes, as she pierced every single one of the servants with a scrutinising look.

"Speak up," she shrieked and pointed to her chair with a dramatic gesture. "Which of you idiotic –"

"It was me," Ebony said with a firm voice and rose from her own chair. "I'm sorry. It must have slipped from my plate when I had an early luncheon. I'm very sorry."

Everyone stared at her with wide eyes. Ebony tried her best to meet the furious gaze of the queen, but it was hard to withstand her look after a while. *Father was right. Whenever one is lying, it's hard to look the other into the eyes …*

"I'm sorry," Ebony repeated with an apologetical look, before she dropped her gaze and stared down at her hands, hoping that her plan would work.

"You'd better be sorry," snarled the queen. "You have ruined one of my best dresses! Now I've got to go and change!"

"Wouldn't you want to eat first?" asked the king with a worried voice and tried to calm his enraged wife. "You could change after luncheon –"

"– and sit here with my ruined dress all the time? No! Definitely not! Maybe it's not too late to do something about the stain. I'd better take the dress off now and see what the damage is."

With that said, the queen departed, still fuming and called her chambermaids to help her out of the dress as quickly as possible.

"Maybe there is still time to save it," Ebony heard the queen say before she and her servants left the long hall.

"Well," said the king with a puzzled look on his face. "That was a nasty turn of events." He turned to Ebony with a stern look. "I truly hope that you'll never do anything like this ever again. It was very childish of you!"

He knows that I was lying!

"I'm sorry, father. I'm sure it will never happen again."

"Good. As a punishment for your bad behaviour, I want you to go to your room right now. If you actually had an early luncheon like you stated, you won't be needing anything to eat until dinner."

Fair as always.

"Yes, father. Might I ask you though, if you could accompany me to my room?"

"And leave Snow White to eat alone? I don't think so!"

"Please? It's really important to me, father."

The king eyed Ebony with a bewildered look on his face. Then he got up and denoted her to follow him.

"I'll be right back," he said to Snow White, who was sitting all alone at the long table now. "You can start without me if you're hungry."

Snow White nodded and waved to the servants that they were allowed to serve the food, while the king marched towards the hallway, Ebony right behind him.

As soon as they had left the hall, Ebony quickened her pace and caught up with the long strides of her father.

"Would you like to confess the truth to me?" he asked, before she could even open her mouth. "Why did you put that beetroot on the queen's chair?"

"Because she always keeps you to herself and I had to talk to you alone."

The king slowed down and looked at Ebony with surprise in his eyes.

"You just wanted to speak with me? But why didn't you say so? You didn't have to annoy the queen –"

"Yes, I did. I don't want her to know what I have to say to you. And she would never leave your side, so I had to chase her away somehow."

"That was not nice of you," the king chided her. "I hope that you're planning to apologise for this later on."

"I already said that I'm sorry!"

"Well, say it again then. I don't want any tension between you and my queen. We're supposed to be a happy family."

"Oh, please! A family?" Ebony answered with dry sarcasm. "She doesn't even care about Snow White or me! She only wants *your* company all day long and completely ignores us."

"That's not fair, Ebony, and you know it," grumbled the king as they reached the door to Ebony's chamber. "She is not your mother and it's not easy for her to deal with the children of another woman. But that doesn't mean that she doesn't care about you."

"Sure." Ebony opened the door to her chamber and waved her father inside. "Anyway, there is something you should know."

The king arched an eyebrow, but followed the invitation and entered Ebony's room.

"Make it quick though," he said, while he had a look around. "I don't want to keep Snow White waiting."

"The length of this conversation depends on whether you believe me or not," Ebony replied firmly.

The king turned to look at her and she could feel her heart beating hard against her growing bosom. *I'd better not mess this up now!*

"Well, I'm listening," said the king with an encouraging smile on his otherwise earnest face.

"The queen is treating the people badly behind your back," Ebony blurted out, before she could organise her thoughts. "When you were away last time, she treated the people and their concerns as if they didn't matter to her at all. She was neither just nor kind and often sent people away without helping them, because she said their wishes were 'petty' and 'not worth of her time'. I think she doesn't really care about the people – only about herself and her beauty."

"That is a heavy accusation," said the king gravely.

All traces of a smile had vanished from his face and he was looking at Ebony with furrowed brows.

"I know," replied Ebony. "But it's the truth!"

The king eyed her with a scrutinising look for a while, as if to determine whether she was lying or not. Ebony met his gaze with equal determination, not wavering for a second. *This time I'm telling the truth! And I'm sure that he knows it. The question is: Can he accept it?*

"Do you have any proof?" the king finally asked after a few seconds of stern silence.

"Only my word and my eyes, which bore witness to all of this. I'm sure the people would tell you the truth as well, if the queen wasn't present at every hearing."

The king mused on this for another couple of seconds. Ebony watched the fight of emotions within his eyes and knew that he didn't want to believe what she was saying. *He'd prefer to stay wrapped in her illusions of kindness and beauty. But he can't keep his eyes closed forever. I'll make him see, even if it is the last thing I do! He has got to know the truth. How else could he ensure the just reign of his kingdom?*

"Alright," the king's voice ripped Ebony out of her thoughts. "I believe you. But without more proof, there is nothing I can do about this. I'll have to see it with my own eyes."

"But father —"

"I'll keep an eye on it, my dear. I promise. But until then, I ask you to keep this to yourself. Don't mention it to Snow White and definitely not to the queen or any of the servants. We'll have to keep this our secret for now."

"Do you want to hush this up??"

"No. I want to find proof. But until then you'll have to trust me and keep quiet about this. Alright?"

"Fine."

I can only hope that he really means it and doesn't want to pretend as if this never happened. I won't keep quiet forever.

"Well, I'd better get back to Snow White then," the king sighed, already lost in thoughts as he turned towards the door.

"Oh, yes! About Snow White," Ebony exclaimed, "there is something else I have to tell you."

The king turned back and looked at Ebony with tired eyes. *Oh dear! Hearing about all this must have been hard on him already. He probably couldn't take it if I told him that his wife might be a witch who's got her eyes on Snow White …*

"What else?" asked the king with a voice that clearly gave away that he wasn't ready for any more bad news.

"Oh, never mind," Ebony said quickly. "It's not that urgent. I wouldn't want for you to miss luncheon."

The king nodded and turned, hurriedly leaving the room as if he was trying to flee from the truth he had just learned. Ebony stayed behind, hungry but satisfied with her work and hoped that her father would stay true to his promise. *He never backs down on his word. He'd better not start now!*

$\mathfrak{At}$ first, it seemed as if nothing had changed. The queen would just ignore Ebony as she had done before and tried to keep the king all to herself again.

As the days grew longer and summer approached, the king spent more time in the gardens though, where Snow White was blooming along with the flowers, dancing through the sun like the butterflies she adored so much.

Ebony on the other hand kept a close watch on the queen and noticed that she would eye Snow White with envy, when she saw her playing hide and seek with the king. *Seems like she dislikes Snow White both for her beauty and her talent to get her father's attention.*

After a while, Ebony noticed that, whenever the queen had watched Snow White play in the gardens, she quickly disappeared into her tower. Ebony didn't dare to sneak into the queen's chambers once more, but she was sure that the queen was checking on her magic mirror, making sure that she was still the fairest of all women in the kingdom.

Time passed and summer came, until the king finally announced that he would be leaving the castle for two weeks, to visit one of the neighbouring kingdoms. As always, he left the queen in charge and parted from her with promises of pretty new dresses.

Ebony watched all that from high up in the castle and wondered what her father was up to. She could sense that he was nervous, as if he was trying to hide something from his wife. *What could be his plan? Has he told any of the servants to keep an eye on her?*

Not being sure whether her father would actually stay true to his word, Ebony decided to watch the actions of the queen herself.

Therefore, she sneaked into the throne room, shortly before the queen and the people were to arrive for the weekly hearing. As she hid behind one of the statues, she noticed a silhouette hidden in the shadow of another statue a bit further down the hall. *I was right! Father did take precautions.*

She tried to make out who the other one was, but she couldn't see his or her face, because the person was wearing a cloak with a hood to hide it.

Ebony didn't have time to wonder who might be hiding under the hood, because at that moment, the queen entered and seated herself upon the throne.

"Bring in the first one," she demanded from the guards at the high doors, who instantly followed her order and brought in the first peasant. "What do you want?"

The hunched man stepped forward with shy eyes and didn't dare to meet the cold gaze of the queen.

"I'm sorry to disturb your highness –"

"Oh, no. But you will be sorry if you waste my time. So be quick and tell me what you want. I don't have all day!"

"Yes, my queen. Of course, my queen. I came here to ask whether the payment of my dues might be postponed a little longer. I haven't managed to make enough profit to pay for the –"

"Why not?"

"I – I – beg your pardon, my queen?"

"Why haven't you made enough profit?"

"I had a bad harvest last time and –"

"This is not my fault, is it?"

"No – No, of course not, your highness."

"Well, I don't see why I should be held responsible for it then. Either you manage to pay your dues and make enough profit by the end of next month or you'll be chased off your property. That'll be all."

"But – my queen – please –"

"Go and beg to someone else for mercy. I have nothing more to say!"

The queen leaned back on the throne and gave the peasant such a menacing look that he hurriedly backed out of the throne room.

Ebony clenched her fists and looked towards the cloaked figure to her left. Whoever he or she was, there was no reaction to be seen within the shadow of the statue.

Taking a deep breath, Ebony kept herself from stepping forward and bore witness to the rest of the procedures instead. They all ended in a similar way, leaving behind devastated or weeping people, who were sent away by the unrelenting queen.

When the last of them left the throne room, the queen got up to leave as well. She had only taken a few steps towards the side door though, when suddenly a booming voice echoed through the room.

"This is how you treat my people?"

Both Ebony and the queen flinched, but in a very different manner. Ebony jerked around to see her father, pulling back the hood and stepping out of the shadows, while the queen jumped and froze to the spot. It took a second before she turned around very slowly to face her grim husband.

"I thought," the queen said with a velvety voice, "you'd be gone for a few days. Didn't you say so?"

"No. I said I'd be gone *for a while* – and I have – but that is not the topic here. How dare you treat my people like dirt? Is this how you repay me for my trust in you?"

This time the king seemed untouched by the queen's dazzling smile and her crooning voice. He stared at her with unforgiving eyes, until she gave up on her smile and met his gaze with her chin held high.

"Well, I might have forgotten my manners today. But it was not my fault. Your daughters are driving me crazy. Snow White has been singing all day long and Ebony is playing tricks on me again. This time she *threw* food at me! I was barely able to escape. She nearly ruined another one of my beautiful dresses!"

The king raised an eyebrow and then turned around towards the stone statue behind which Ebony was hiding.

"Is this true, Ebony?"

Ebony gulped, but stepped forward into the light and met her father's gaze with an earnest look, trying to ignore the evil stare the queen was giving her.

"No, father. It is not true. I have done no such thing and neither has Snow White. She's merely been singing in the garden, as always, which can hardly drive anyone mad inside the castle."

Ebony darted a glance at the queen, but hurriedly turned towards her father again. *Why can't he see that she's pure evil inside? Anyone who met those eyes right now would instantly have to believe that she's a witch!*

Her father didn't seem to reach the same conclusion. When he looked from Ebony to the queen, the latter had already clothed her face in smiles again, trying to win over his affection.

"Do you really believe your daughter instead of me?" she asked, fluttering her long eyelashes. "She's just a child."

"I do believe the one who tells the truth," answered the king and peered at the queen with searching eyes. "Have you been telling me the truth, my love?"

The queen met his gaze and smiled innocently.

"Of course, I have. I'd never lie to you, my love!"

"Wouldn't you?"

The king kept his eyes locked with hers, until her smile started to waver a bit. The hint of a blush rosed her cheeks and she finally tore her eyes away from the king, only to look daggers at Ebony, who flinched, but didn't look away.

"You put your daughters before me?" shrieked the queen all of a sudden and pointed at Ebony, her eyes flaring with rage. "*She* is the gloomy one. Always brooding and speaking ill of others. If you have to mistrust anyone, it should be her – *not me!* This is absurd. I'm the queen. Why do I have to give account for my behaviour, while your children get away with anything?"

"You have to give account, *because* you are the queen," the king said insistently. "You hold great responsibility, my love, and I have to know whether I can trust you or not."

"Of course, you can!"

"Then why do you lie to me and maltreat my people?"

"I never lied to you. Ebony did, didn't she? She put those stories about me being a bad queen inside your head! She is trying to get rid of me, because she wants you all to herself. She can't accept that you love me more than her!"

"I don't," objected the king. "I love you all the same, each in their own way. You are all very dear to me, which is exactly why I don't want you to hate each other."

"She started it!" yelled the queen, pointing at Ebony again. "She ruined my dress, remember?"

"Yes, but if I recall it correctly, she apologised for that several times. And I've bought you new dresses since then. You hardly have too few of them, have you?"

"That's not the point –"

"Exactly. The point is: Why did you treat my people so badly today? Was it an exception? Or have you done this before?"

"No! It was only due to my bad mood. I can't stand Snow White's high voice all day long. And those gloomy looks from Ebony! It drives me mad."

"That is no excuse for taking it out on the people," argued the king. "I will forgive you this time, but I don't want this to happen ever again. Have I made myself clear?"

"Yes, my love."

"Good. Let's give the people an apology then."

"What?!"

The queen eyed her husband with wide eyes, while he approached his throne and sat upon it, giving his cloak to one of the servants and calling for a chair.

"Ebony, come and sit by my side, will you?"

Ebony followed her father's invitation, similarly puzzled as the queen, who sat down on her throne to the right of the king and tried to look as dignified as possible.

"But I already dealt with all of them," the queen said with an air of confusion.

"I know," replied the king. "I've seen it. But I told the guards in advance that they were to keep the people inside the castle for a possible second hearing."

"But – why?! What is this? Didn't you trust me in the first place?"

"Let's say that I've heard rumours," the king just said and called for the people to be let in. "And now listen closely how I want matters to be handled."

From this day forth, Ebony was present for every single one of the weekly hearings. The queen would attend them, too, listening to her husband's judgements with a stony face and an icy gaze, which none of the people dared to meet.

Ebony, on the other hand, felt rather victorious and enjoyed spending time with her father. Sometimes, after a hearing, he'd spend half an hour with her, explaining to her why he had handled matters the way he did.

The queen never stayed for those 'lectures' of course. Sometimes she even skipped the weekly hearings, saying that she didn't feel well and then she brooded inside her chambers instead.

Whenever she met Ebony alone in a hallway, she'd look at her in such a menacing way that Ebony hurried on and out of sight as quickly as possible. She would have feared for her life at times, if she hadn't known that her father would protect her. *She can't hurt me while I'm within the reach of his protection. If she tried to murder me in my sleep, my father would surely hear it. His chamber is not far away from Snow White's and mine.*

And still, Ebony couldn't help having the feeling that she had awakened something evil within the queen. She looked more pale than usual and lost her temper more often than before. It was as if her mask of beauty had cracked and now that her evil side was shining through, she wasn't able to hide it anymore.

Even the servants were frightened of her tempers and avoided entering the south tower, never going in there alone or after dusk.

A whole year passed in that manner and only the king seemed to be untouched by the changes in the atmosphere within the castle. He acted as if every problem was solved, even though he didn't visit any of the other kingdoms for quite a while.

When he finally did, he left one of his trusted men in charge of the throne room, who also attended the weekly hearings – together with Ebony – and kept an eye on the queen.

She still wasn't as kind as the king, but tried her best to act more just, so that there would be nothing bad to report about her.

After a while, Ebony started to relax a little and when winter came, her worries about the evil inside the queen were washed away by her enthusiasm for the first snow. From then on, she spent most of her time outside, far away from the evil eyes of the queen, who wouldn't go out into the cold.

That way, Ebony forgot to tell her father about what she had seen within the secret chamber and even started to forget her own worries about the queen being a witch.

Thus, when she and Snow White turned fourteen, Ebony didn't worry about the growing femineity and charm of her older sister, who was turning into a lovely young woman with well-proportioned feminine curves.

Even Ebony grew prettier during the winter, but she stayed a bit skinnier than Snow White and had a rather flat bosom, which didn't bother her though. *This way, I can make sure that no one will marry me for my good looks, but rather for my sharp mind. If anyone ever wants to marry me at all that is …*

So far, all the princes who had attended a ball at their castle had been mesmerised by Snow White's beauty and tender heart only and had barely looked at Ebony.

The older men had always admired the ethereal beauty of the queen, which the latter had enjoyed very much, despite having the king at her side.

As soon as his daughters had turned sixteen, the king was planning a grand ball for the coming summer, Snow White's favourite time of the year. The two princesses were both looking forward to meeting new people and Snow White was starting to design her own flowery dress, with which she wanted to impress the princes which were to attend the ball.

"Maybe we'll meet the love of our lives," Snow White raved, while she showed Ebony the sketches for her ball dress, which she had created with her personal dressmaker. "Wouldn't that be wonderful?"

"I don't know," Ebony replied with a critical look. "How would you know that it's him?"

"I'll just know. It's like magic! The moment you look at him and he looks at you, you'll feel it. Love at first sight! That's what I want for myself. Don't you?"

"I'm not sure if you can really love someone at first sight," Ebony wondered sceptically. "It would be very superficial, wouldn't it? Just falling in love with the good looks of the other? Don't you want to get to know him first and see whether his character is as beautiful as his face?"

"No," Snow White fluted and danced through the room in the arms of an imaginary prince. "I just want someone who loves and adores me."

Ebony shook her head and gave up on debating about love with her sister. *It's a hopeless case. Her mind seems to be fixed on the idea of love at first sight way too much! I can't argue with that.*

While winter turned into spring, the castle was starting to be filled with excitement about the upcoming ball. The king had invited kings and queens from all over the world and each of them would bring their children along. There was a lot of food to be prepared and stored for the big feast and the servants were busy planning it all, while the first buds started to bloom in the castle gardens.

"There'll be a hundred princes and princesses," rejoiced Snow White one evening, when their father had told them, that all the invitations had been accepted. "Can you imagine that, Ebby? All those beautiful dresses? I'll have to work really hard to bring mine to perfection if I want to find my one true love. And I have designed one for you as well. Mine is dark red with white flowers and yours is emerald green with white feathers. That way our dresses will go together beautifully and will be the highlight of the ball!"

Ebony shared her sister's excitement, even though she didn't care much about the dresses. She was more interested in the different cultures and customs of the people who would attend their ball.

"Maybe they'll have completely different ways of dancing than we do," she mused and took Snow White by the hands to whirl her around.

"Oh, that would be fun," giggled Snow White and put her hand upon Ebony's shoulder, while they danced through one of the great halls. "Maybe we should make up a dance of our own, which we could teach to them."

"Wonderful idea! One with lots of whirls and liftings."

The two sisters laughed and started to sing a song to which they improvised a whole dance routine, at the end of which Ebony actually managed to lift up Snow White.

"You'd make a fine prince," Snow White nagged her and put out her hand for Ebony to kiss.

"At your service, your highness," replied Ebony with a grin and kissed the hand of her big sister. "Would you do me the honour of dancing with me again?"

"Sure. But first we've got to get something to eat. It's lunchtime and I'm starving!"

They both laughed out loud and turned to leave for the dining hall. Out of the corner of her eye, Ebony thought that she saw someone, watching them from the shadows behind a curtain, but when she looked closer, there was only an empty wall and a closed side door.

As spring proceeded, the flowers of the castle garden all bloomed and flourished, filling the air with their sweet scent.

Snow White spent so much time outside that she started to have the pleasant scent of roses upon her and Ebony often buried her nose within the long black hair of her big sister, when they lay side by side in the lush grass.

"You smell like a bouquet of flowers!"

"So what?" asked Snow White. "It'll only help to impress my one true love – if I should meet him at the ball."

"Why wouldn't you? Princes from all lands are coming to this ball. You'll never get a better chance than this one. I'm sure that you'll find the love of your life."

"Really?" Snow White turned towards Ebony and eyed her with sisterly affection. "I'll miss you, you know? When I marry my prince and move to another kingdom –"

"I'll miss you, too, big sis! Even though my nose wouldn't mind getting a break from this intense smell of roses once in a while."

"As if! I'm sure you'll miss it once I'm gone."

"Maybe. But if I want to feel close to you, I can always bury my nose within the rose bushes. Even though it's a bit pricklier than you are."

"I'm not prickly at all," exclaimed Snow White and nudged her sister into the arm. "I'm as soft and smooth as a rose petal. That's what mother always used to say."

They both sighed and stared up into the sky, wondering if their mother was up there somewhere, watching over them from a place within the clouds.

Little did they know that there actually was a whole castle within the clouds, even though it was not their mother who watched them from there, but the old Good Fairy and her young apprentice.

And someone else was watching them.

The envious queen was peering out of her window, eyeing the two princesses with malice. She didn't care much about Ebony, though she hated her for having unmasked her in front of the king. But it was Snow White whom she loathed the most. The very sight of the older princess, who was growing more beautiful by the day, was like a thorn in the queen's heart, which tormented her day and night.

One day, as the queen couldn't stand watching the two princesses in the garden anymore, she went up to her magic mirror instead, hoping to be appeased by his reassuring words.

"Mirror, mirror, on the wall, who is the fairest of us all?"

"You are fair, my queen, no doubt. But Snow White is the fairest one about."

"What?!" shrieked the queen so loud that the glass of the magic mirror rattled. "That cannot be! It's a lie!"

"I don't lie," answered the magic mirror truthfully.

"But this can't be true. That little brat cannot be more beautiful than me. No one can! It's not fair. My beauty is all I have! Why would she get all the love and attention? I'm the queen, she is nothing!"

There was no answer to that.

The queen tried once more to ask the question, which normally gave her so much satisfaction, but the answer was the same: Snow White was the fairest one of all.

Rage and envy bubbled up inside the queen's heart and let it pump the blood through her body with such a force that her face turned red with anger. She walked back and forth through her secret chamber, until anger turned into cold fury and whitened her face till it was as pale as a sheet.

"I can't let this happen," the queen finally mumbled. "If Snow White gets all the attention at the ball, I'll burst with anger. I can't take it! The world may never know about her beauty. I'll have to get rid of her before the ball. No one shall ever lay eyes on her again!"

For a few days, the queen brooded over this problem, while Snow White and Ebony were having their dresses made ready for the approaching ball. There were only a few weeks left and feelings ran high within the castle. Everybody was busy and organising some part of the event.

Even the king was getting excited, hoping to find a suiting husband for each of his daughters. To make sure that they would stand out of the crowd, he left the castle five days prior to the ball, to buy new necklaces for both of them.

Snow White was thrilled about this, because she loved sparkly things and jewellery very much.

Ebony on the other hand was more interested in the preparations of the feast and spent some time in the great kitchen, watching and smelling the food which was arranged.

That way, she didn't notice the bad mood of the queen, nor the smile upon the queen's face when the king told them that he would leave the castle for a few days.

The day he left, Ebony went into the kitchen once more, eager to learn more about spices and herbs, while Snow White went out into the garden to play among the flowers.

She was just chasing a few butterflies through the rose bushes, as one of the huntsmen approached her with grim eyes and a blank face.

"Would you like to go for a ride?" he asked nervously, trying not to meet her eyes. "There are some beautiful flowers within the forest nearby that the queen asked me to show to you."

"How nice of her," replied Snow White with a beaming smile. "But father left with the carriage –"

"Yes, but your horse is ready and could use some exercise, my lady," answered the huntsman and led the princess through a secret passageway that ended right at the edge of the forest.

Snow White didn't notice the shaking hands of the huntsman as he helped her onto the horse and neither did she see the nervous glances he was casting at her from time to time.

They rode into the forest, unnoticed by Ebony and the servants, as everyone was busy with the preparations for the ball.

Snow White chattered away happily, not minding the silence of the huntsman, who didn't dare to speak a word. Because what the princess didn't know was that the poor man had been given orders by the queen to murder Snow White and burry her deep within the woods, where no one would ever find her.

When they reached a rather dark part of the forest, the huntsman stopped and dismounted his horse, signalling Snow White to do the same.

"The flowers are over there. But we should leave the horses behind or else they'll step onto the pretty blossoms and ruin them."

"Of course," agreed Snow White and followed the huntsman without fear or doubt.

When they had walked for a few minutes though, she started to get confused, because there were still no flowers to be seen.

"Are you sure that we're walking into the right direction?" she asked the huntsman and turned around.

Only then did she notice that he had stopped several paces behind her and was now holding a dagger in his shaking hands.

"Oh!" the princess exclaimed, taking a step back. "Is something the matter?"

"Poor child," sighed the huntsman. "I'm afraid that the queen has ordered me to kill you."

"What? No! That can't be –"

"I'm speaking the truth, my lady."

"But why? What have I done?"

"She didn't tell me the reason," admitted the huntsman. "She only told me to kill and bury you here within the woods and bring back your heart, as proof that you are truly dead."

"But this is awful," Snow White cried out and started to sob. "I beg of you – please don't kill me. Have mercy upon me, dear huntsman."

"I'm sorry, my child, but the queen will kill me if I defy her orders."

He stepped forward, the dagger at the ready. Snow White broke into tears and stumbled backwards, while she lifted up her hands as if to shield herself from harm.

"Please," she begged. "I promise that I'll run away and never return to the castle. The queen will never know that I'm still alive. But please, don't kill me. Have mercy!"

The huntsman stopped and looked at the weeping princess. Even with tears rolling down her cheeks, the beauty of her was undeniable and her pleading words touched his heart.

"Alright. I'll spare your life. But you have to stay true to your word and never come back to the castle. Otherwise, we'll both be doomed."

"I'll never come back," promised Snow White with a shaking voice. "Thank you, noble man. I owe you my life."

With that, she turned and ran into the woods as fast as her graceful feet would take her.

The huntsman stayed behind and watched her disappear behind the trees, until he was sure that she was gone. Then he turned around and rode back towards the castle, looking out for a deer or boar whom he might kill so that he would have a heart to take back to the queen.

Luck was on his side and he slayed an innocent animal to provide a heart that he showed to the queen as he got back, claiming that it was Snow White's and that she was dead.

The queen grinned and ate the heart for dinner, celebrating her victory upon Snow White, while the latter was still dashing through the forest.

It was getting dark and Snow White was tired from running. Also the darkness frightened her, because it made her stumble over tree roots and was filled by eerie sounds which seemed to surround her, as if the dark forces of the queen were still trying to hunt her down.

Just as she was about to succumb to her fears, she spotted a light in the distance. New hope swelling up inside her heart, she stumbled forward, towards the light and soon came upon a small hut, which was surrounded by bushes and flowers.

There was a tidy vegetable patch in front of the house and the light inside shone bright and comforting.

"Hello?" Snow White called out and knocked on the door of the small hut. "Is anyone home?"

There was no answer, but upon her third knock, the door swung open a little and the princess peeked inside to see whether she might spot the owner of the house.

"Hello?" she called out again, but there was only silence inside the small hut. "I'm coming inside now."

With careful steps, making sure to clean her shoes before stepping onto the wooden floor, Snow White entered the hut and looked around.

There was a tiny kitchen and a small living area, with a table which was already laid out for seven people. Each plate and piece of furniture seemed to be of miniature size as if the house was inhabited by children only.

"They must be very small people," Snow White said to herself while she went forward to the table and eyed the food with a grumbling stomach. "I wonder when they will get back?"

She decided to wait a little longer and first had a look around the house, before she returned to the table. There was still no sign of anyone to return at all and thus she decided to satisfy her grumbling stomach with a bit of food and drink from the table.

To avoid upsetting the owners of the hut, she only took a tiny piece of each of the seven plates though, biting off just a small bit of bread and cheese. The same she did with the wine and water, only taking a sip from each of the seven wooden jugs.

As soon as she had eaten, her tired body demanded some rest. She had already discovered a bedroom with seven small beds and picked the biggest of them, onto which she curled up and instantly fell asleep, not noticing how the seven inhabitants of the hut finally got home late in the evening.

They were astonished to find that someone had eaten from their table, but when they spotted the sleeping princess within their bedroom, they were charmed by her beauty and didn't wake her up until the next morning.

It was quite a surprise to Snow White as she woke up to the clatter und buzz of the seven dwarves – because it was them who owned the hut – getting ready for breakfast.

She blushed when she stepped into the kitchen and found herself surrounded by the tiny dwarves, which were about the size of a child.

"Good morning," they greeted her with friendly voices and the oldest of them stepped forward. "We didn't mean to wake you up. You looked like you needed the rest."

"Thank you all so very much," replied Snow White with a humble smile which warmed their hearts. "I'm very sorry that I entered your house uninvited and ate some of your food. I hope you can forgive me."

"We can indeed," answered the dwarves as one. "But who are you and how did you get here?"

Snow White told them her name and how she had ended up deep within the forest with no place to live and no home to return to.

The dwarves were touched by her story and her charming voice, just as much as they were horrified by the cruelty of the queen.

"That's an evil witch," one of the dwarves exclaimed when Snow White had finished her tale. "You should make sure never to cross paths with her again."

"You could stay with us," suggested another dwarf and eyed the beautiful princess with hopeful eyes. "We wouldn't mind your company."

"Are you sure?" asked Snow White, who couldn't believe her luck and was very grateful for the kindness of the seven dwarves.

"Of course," they all cried out. "You're welcome to stay with us as long as you want. Just make sure that you don't let anyone in while we're gone to work in the mines, in case the evil queen comes looking for you. She might find out that you're still alive and probably will try to kill you again."

"I'll make sure to look out for her or the huntsman," promised Snow White. "And I'll clean your clothes, wash your dishes and take care of your garden – if you can show me how to do it. That's the least I can do for you to repay you for your kindness."

The dwarves agreed to this and thus it was settled: Snow White was to stay with them, out of the reach of the evil queen, who would hopefully never find her.

Ebony became suspicious right away when Snow White didn't show up for dinner. Her older sister was always the first at the table, having a healthy appetite and never missing a meal.

Thus, she was very worried not to find her in the dining hall and quite confused when not even the queen would show up for dinner.

"The queen prefers to eat in her own chambers today," explained one of the servants as Ebony asked them about the whereabouts of the missing women. "And your sister hasn't shown up yet."

"Is she not in her room?" asked Ebony with worry in her voice. "She can't be in the garden. It's getting dark already."

"I'll send someone to look for her," reassured the servant and scuttled off in a hurry.

Snow White was not in her room though and not to be found in the castle gardens either. Ebony didn't want to start dinner without her sister and instead went looking for her as well.

Soon the whole castle was filled with servants, running along the hallways and calling out the name of the eldest princess.

"Where are you, big sis?" Ebony mumbled to herself while she circled the castle for the second time. "Why would you miss dinner?"

Neither answers nor Snow White could be found anywhere. It seemed as if the princess had just disappeared. Ebony was getting more worried by the hour and stayed up until late in the night, without even thinking of eating.

She finally went to bed, exhausted and with a grumbling stomach. Worry kept her awake for quite a while, but tiredness won in the end and let her fall into a restless sleep, with nightmares about dragons and trolls, who captured and abducted her older sister into the woods.

When Ebony woke up in the morning, she didn't remember her dreams, but the fear stayed within her heart, gripping it with icy fingers which didn't want to let go again.

As soon as she had dressed, Ebony ran towards her sister's bedroom and hoped with all might that everything had just been a bad dream.

Snow White wasn't there though and reality crushed all of Ebony's hopes when she reached the dining hall, which was empty and cold as well. *Snow White would never miss dinner AND breakfast. Only if she would be very sick! But then she'd be in her bedroom …*

At this moment, the door opened and Ebony yanked up her head, her heart beating faster. It was the queen who entered though and the smug look on her face gave Ebony the chills.

"Good morning," the queen fluted, her eyes sparkling with victorious happiness. "Isn't it a beautiful day?"

Ebony stared at the queen with wide eyes, while the latter sat down at the table and instantly demanded for breakfast to be served.

"Shouldn't we wait for Snow White?" Ebony asked and watched the queen's reaction very closely.

"Why wait? She knows where we are, doesn't she? If she wanted to join us, she would be here already."

The evil glint inside the queen's cold eyes made Ebony's hair stand on end. *I've never seen her look so cheerful! Could she have something to do with Snow White's disappearance?*

Ebony willed herself to sit down and force some of the breakfast into her mouth, while she watched the queen from the corner of her eye. There was definitely an air of happiness about her, which hadn't been there before. It made her look more beautiful again, as if Snow White's absence only added to the queen's looks.

When the queen was finished, she went back towards her chambers, silently being followed by Ebony, who couldn't get rid of her suspicion anymore.

Casting her fear aside, Ebony even dared to follow the queen into her chambers, as soon as she was sure that she wouldn't be spotted. She sneaked up the staircase, listening for a sound that would give away the whereabouts of the queen. *Maybe she has imprisoned Snow White in one of her rooms and is trying to transfer my sister's beauty to her herself with some dark magic.*

Ebony's heart was beating fast when she finally reached the top of the south tower and peeked into the secret chamber. The door stood ajar a little and enabled her to watch the queen, who was standing in front of the magic mirror.

"Mirror, mirror, on the wall, who is the fairest of us all?"

"You are the fairest here, my queen. But Snow White is still the fairest to be seen."

"What?! No! There's got to be a mistake."

"I don't make mistakes," responded the magic mirror.

"But she's dead!" shrieked the queen. "Snow White is dead! I ate her heart. I know that she's dead!"

Ebony shrunk back. The words of the queen seemed to pierce her own heart, which felt like it might burst into a million pieces at any moment. *Snow White is dead?*

"The huntsman killed her for me," the queen ranted on, while her face went red with anger again. "He wouldn't dare to defy my orders! He brought me her heart."

Ebony recoiled and started to move away from the door with silent steps. Her head felt as if she was in a daze and the rush of her blood let her ears go numb. *I was right. The queen did it.* Another step back and Ebony reached the stone steps. *She ordered the huntsman to kill Snow White so that she would be the fairest again.* Another step, down the staircase. Her heart was racing and her feet urged her to pick up the pace too.

Still unable to blink or think straight, Ebony turned around and fled down the stone steps, out of the south tower and the queen's chamber. She didn't even care whether she was seen anymore. She just wanted to get away from the evil queen as fast as possible. *She killed Snow White! No. Wait. She gave the order. But the huntsman – which huntsman? Anyway, one of them killed Snow White! I've got to find him and …*

Ebony wasn't sure what she would do if she found out who murdered her sister. She just kept running, until she reached the sleeping quarters of the king's huntsmen. There she stopped dead, unsure what to do next.

While she was trying to think of a way to unmask the murderer of her sister, her thoughts, without being asked, returned towards the secret chamber. And then it struck her. *Snow White's got to be alive! The magic mirror said so himself. And if it's true that he doesn't make mistakes – that's got to mean that Snow White wasn't killed after all!*

Once more, her heart started to race, but this time it was jubilating. Encouraged by her new hope, Ebony burst into the sleeping quarters and met the gaze of a dozen startled men, who luckily were all dressed.

"Which of you went to see Snow White yesterday?"

Dead silence filled the room.

"Um ... Pardon me, my lady," one of the huntsmen said. "But why would any of us come to see your sister?"

"Never mind," Ebony blurted out. "Which one of you was it? Who spoke to her yesterday?"

Her eyes quickly scanned the faces of all the men, who were eyeing her with astonishment and curiosity. Every one of them met her gaze without hesitation, all except one. He was trying to hide at the back of the room, avoiding her searching gaze and looking down upon his hands instead.

"You!" Ebony exclaimed with a commanding voice, making all of the huntsmen jump. "You there, at the back. Follow me."

The huntsman looked up with fear in his eyes, but didn't dare to ignore her order. He went pale when he got up and followed her into the courtyard, too nervous to ask where she was taking him.

Ebony made sure to take a path that couldn't be watched from the south tower and walked at a quick pace, leading the nervous huntsman towards the back of one of the horse stables.

There she spun around, making him flinch, and eyed him with a scrutinising gaze.

"What's your name?"

"Henry, my lady."

"Well, Henry. Speak the truth!" she commanded with a stern voice. "Did you go to see Snow White yesterday?"

"Yes," answered the huntsman, while he gripped his belt so tightly that his knuckles went white.

"Who ordered you to see her?"

"I can't tell you, my lady."

"Why not?"

"Well –"

The huntsman looked down at his hands, lost for words.

"Why not?" repeated Ebony insistently.

"I'm not allowed to, my lady."

"Who forbid you to talk about it? Was it the queen?"

The head of the huntsman shot up, his eyes widened by fear and his face as pale as Ebony's.

"How did you know that? Are you here to question me on her behalf?"

"Don't be silly! I'm not the one following orders of the queen here. But you did, didn't you? You took Snow White away and were supposed to kill her. That's what happened, isn't it?"

The huntsman nodded, not trusting his voice to speak.

"But you didn't kill her," Ebony stated and watched the reaction of the huntsman.

He was still as pale as snow and his eyes widened, while they tried to meet her gaze, but failed and looked upon his shaking hands instead.

"Did you kill her or not?" asked Ebony with a firm voice.

"I – I – I couldn't," stammered Henry will a lump in his throat. "She begged me for mercy and her – her speech and beauty touched me. She was crying and I – I pitied her."

"You let her go then?"

"Yes."

The huntsman looked down at the ground as if this confession had been his death sentence.

Ebony on the other hand let out a sigh of relief, but then her brows furrowed again.

"You were touched by her beauty, huh? You wouldn't have been merciful on me then, would you? Because I'm not beautiful? Would you have followed the queen's orders if it had been me instead of Snow White?"

"I guess that depends on the speech you would have given. If it would have softened my heart as much as your sister's –"

"But apart from the speech – would my looks keep you from killing me? Would they make you pity me?"

The huntsman eyed Ebony for a second, until he quickly looked down upon his hands again and shook his head.

"I'm afraid not, my lady. Right now, your dark eyes are rather intimidating. They make you look like a wild animal. And I kill those all the time."

"I see." A bitter smile spread over Ebony's face. "Well, I guess I'm lucky that it wasn't me who was supposed to be killed. But about my sister: Where did you take her? And where is she now?"

"I don't know, my lady. I took her deep into the woods, just as the queen had commanded me to do, but then I let Snow White run away instead of killing her. She might have gone anywhere."

"Do you think she would have survived the night?"

The huntsman didn't dare to answer that question, because he was sure that the answer would be 'no'. Ebony on the other hand was determined to get her sister back and thus forced herself to believe that there was some chance for survival within the woods – even for a fragile princess who had been spoiled by her father and didn't know anything about surviving in the wild. *She's got to be alive! I can't lose her as well. It would be like losing a part of myself. And her brown eyes are all I have left from my mother. I have to find her!*

$\mathfrak{Just}$ as much as no one had noticed that Snow White was riding off with the huntsman, no one seemed to care about Ebony's whereabouts either.

While the servants were still running through the castle, searching for the older princess, the younger one was getting her horse ready and took off unnoticed by anyone but the guards at the gate.

Henry had been very willing to accompany her as soon as Ebony had warned him that the queen had found out that Snow White was still alive. He took all his belongings with him and swore to himself to flee to another kingdom, as soon as he had shown Ebony the place where he had last seen Snow White.

"And she went into that direction?" asked Ebony, looking towards the wilderness to which Henry was pointing.

"Yes, my lady," replied the huntsman with a sad look on his face. "I'm sorry if I can't help you any further, but if what you told me is true, I'd better make sure to get away from the queen as far as possible."

"Of course. I hope you can escape the queen's wrath, Henry. And thank you again for sparing my sister's life." *Even though you might not have spared mine.*

"Thank you, my lady. And good luck to you as well."

With that, they parted and Ebony rode on in the direction that the huntsman had pointed out to her, while he rode off towards the road to one of the neighbouring kingdoms.

At the same time the king returned from his journey, bringing with him two marvellous necklaces for his two daughters. But when he reached the castle, it weren't the happy faces of the princesses who greeted him. Instead, there were worried servants all over the place, running here and there, despair within their eyes and fear within their voices.

"What is going on?" the king demanded to know when he had gotten into the castle and watched the weird running about for a while.

"Oh, your highness," cried one of the chambermaids. "It's awful! Snow White has gone missing since yesterday evening. And now Ebony is missing as well! She must have gone to search for her sister."

All colour left the king's face as he stared at his servants with blank eyes.

"Both my daughters – gone?"

"Yes, your highness. And not a trace of them left."

"Have you searched in the villages nearby?"

"No, not yet. We've searched the castle grounds a hundred times, but without success."

"We'll search the villages then," the king declared, turning on his heals and calling for his horse. "We'll search the whole kingdom if we have to!"

As the king reached the gate, one of the guards told him that Ebony had ridden off towards the forest in the company of the huntsman. Thus, the king was off again, before the queen had even noticed his return.

She was still in a rage, trying to think of a way to kill Snow White for good. The magic mirror had told her that the princess was living with seven dwarves somewhere deep within the woods and that's where her vengeful thoughts went to.

"I could send someone to kill her," she mused in front of her mirror. "But none of the huntsmen. They aren't any good! Maybe one of the castle guards? But they are too loyal to the king. No, it shouldn't be anyone from the castle.

A man from the village? But he might be charmed by her beauty and would fail the task, just as the stupid huntsman did. I'll kill him for that if I ever lay eyes on him again! Which gives me an idea … Maybe I have to be the one to kill her. I won't be baffled by her looks! Yes, it's got to be me. I'll disguise myself and make sure that she ends up dead – this time for good!"

While the queen left her secret chamber and went to find a good disguise for herself, the king and his men entered the forest and started to search for the two princesses. The tracks of Ebony's horse had been wiped out by those of the animals of the woods though and thus the king went into the wrong direction, finding nothing but deer and squirrels.

Ebony had the same problem with tracking the footprints of her sister and soon was lost within the vast forest, without food or water to keep her mind nurtured. Around midday, her head started to feel dizzy and it was getting hard to concentrate on the direction.

Ebony looked for a stream or small lake, but found nothing of the sort. Her horse kept wandering around amongst the trees, until Ebony was too exhausted to keep her eyes open. Dehydrated, hungry and tired, she lay on the back of her horse, which decided on its own that it was time to go home as soon as the sun went down in the west.

The king and his men returned to the castle at dusk, empty-handed and downcast. Soon after, Ebony's horse brought her back to the castle gate and the guards quickly informed the king about his daughter's arrival.

Ebony, not having eaten for two days and lacking water as well, had collapsed upon the back of the horse and was unconscious when the king hurried into the courtyard.

The guards helped him to get her down from her horse and the king took her into his arms, tears of relief streaming down his bearded face.

"Thank goodness. At least *you* came back to me."

Deep in his heart, a part of him wished that it had been Snow White who had returned to him instead, but he didn't allow this thought to cloud his mind.

He carried Ebony back to her room, where the servants made sure that she woke up and drank something, before she dozed off again.

The king went to see the queen in the meantime, demanding to know what had happened while he was gone.

"Oh," cried the queen with contrived sadness. "It was awful, my dear! One second, I saw Snow White running through the gardens and chasing butterflies and the next second, she was gone!"

"And why didn't you send the guards to look for her in the villages nearby?"

"I didn't think that she would leave the castle grounds. Snow White was never the adventurous type. Why would she run away?"

That was a question which bothered the king for the rest of the night. He walked through his chambers, restless and sleepless, trying to figure out why and where Snow White might have gone to.

He still hadn't found an answer when his tiredness took a toll on him and made him lie down for a few hours, just until dawn.

The queen on the other hand was busy within her chambers, brewing a magic potion which would make Ebony forget the events of the last day.

"I can't have her telling anybody what she knows about the incident," she mumbled to herself, while she stirred the bubbling liquid within her cauldron. "That nosy brat always meddles in affairs that she shouldn't even know about! But I'll teach her a lesson. It's the least I can do if I can't get rid of her yet. It wouldn't be wise to kill her with poison. The king is suspicious enough as it is."

When the potion was ready, the queen brought it to Ebony's chamber and told the chambermaid that it was a special tea to make the princess feel better. And sure enough, as Ebony woke up and tasted the steaming beverage, she suddenly looked a lot less stressed and worried.

Little did the chambermaid know that this was only due to the magic within the potion, which had wiped out Ebony's memory of the last day. Whenever she tried to remember what she had done, a cloudy vastness filled her mind. She couldn't recall the conversation with Henry, nor what she had heard the queen say within her secret chamber.

Instead, when the king visited Ebony's sickbed, she asked him why he looked so worried.

"I thought I'd lost you both!" exclaimed the king and sat down beside her. "Do you have any idea where Snow White might have gone to?"

"Snow White is missing?" Ebony furrowed her brows. "Oh. Yes. I remember. She wasn't there for dinner – I think I went looking for her. But I don't remember where –"

"You were lost in the woods," explained the king with worry on his face. "When your horse returned to the castle, you were unconscious and – at first, I thought – But now you're back!"

"And what about Snow White?" asked Ebony with a puzzled look on her face. "Hasn't she come back yet?"

"No." The king sighed. "No one knows where she went. The castle guards didn't see her leave. I don't even understand why she would leave in the first place. Did she mention anything to you?"

"Not that I can remember," Ebony mused dreamily. "She was in the garden the last time I saw her, practising her dancing skills so that she might impress the princes at the ball."

"Oh dear! The ball. It's too late to call it off now. There are only two days left and the first guests will start to arrive tomorrow."

"But what about Snow White?"

"We'll have to continue searching for her in secret. No one shall know that she is missing. We'll tell everyone that she is sick."

"But why can't we ask the other kings and queens for help? Maybe we could all search together –"

"No. They must not know. They wouldn't trust me to keep their children safe, if I tell them that my own daughters went missing within these very grounds."

Ebony didn't like the idea of keeping Snow White's disappearance a secret, but the king made her promise not to tell anyone about it. Deep down, Ebony was sure that she knew who was responsible for all this, but whenever she tried to concentrate on it, her thoughts wandered off and her mind went dizzy, until she forgot about it all again.

When the day of the ball finally arrived, no one in the castle was in a mood for a feast. Snow White hadn't been found yet and Ebony was acting rather strange, daydreaming most of the time and not being able to concentrate on any given task.

The king made sure though that she remembered her promise to keep Snow White's disappearance a secret and announced at the beginning of the ball that his older daughter had fallen sick.

"She won't be able to attend the dance, but maybe she can hear us singing and laughing. Let us all enjoy this day and dance until our shoes fall off."

At those words, the musicians started to play and soon, everyone was dancing and enjoying themselves. Ebony couldn't help but feel sorry for Snow White, while she looked at all the colours and dresses, which were swirling through the room. *I wish you could have seen this, big sis. I'm wearing the green dress you designed for me. And I have to admit that it goes well with my red hair and the white feathers. I bet yours would have been a feast for the eyes even more! Where are you now?*

"May I ask for this dance?"

A tall, blonde prince stood in front of Ebony and offered his hand to her. *He wants to dance with ME?*

"Yes, of course," Ebony replied with a polite smile and followed him onto the dance floor.

"You are the younger daughter of the king, right?" the prince started a conversation as soon as they were moving over the polished floor.

"Yes, I am. My name is Ebony. And you are –?"

"Prince Edward, at your service."

"Nice to meet you, prince Edward."

They glided through the hall for a while, lost in their own thoughts, until the tall prince spoke again.

"It's a pity that your sister couldn't join us today. I've heard a lot about her. Is it true that she is the most beautiful woman all around?"

I knew it! He just wanted to dance with me to ask questions about Snow White. Even when she's not here, she is still the centre of attention.

"I'm sure that she is," replied Ebony, even though she couldn't tell why she was so certain about this. "At least I definitely think she's beautiful."

"A shame that she can't be here with us," sighed prince Edward sadly. "What kind of sickness has befallen her? I hope it's not too serious –"

"My father doesn't want me to talk about her. My mother always used to say that it's rude to talk about people during their absence."

"Oh. I see."

Prince Edward gave up upon the topic and soon seemed to lose his interest in Ebony. As soon as they finished their dance, he excused himself and went away to talk to a group of other young men, which were eyeing Ebony with curiosity. *I guess they're all disappointed that they have to put up with me instead of Snow White. The tales about her beauty must have spread wide and far throughout the years. And now she's gone – but where to?*

No one asked Ebony for a dance for quite a while and she was lost within the dizzying thoughts which clouded her mind. A part of her noticed how the queen was admired by most of the kings and lords, while the foreign princes and princesses danced and laughed together. *I should be enjoying myself as well. This ball was planned in honour of my birthday too. I'm sure Snow White would want me to enjoy it for the both of us – wherever she is … Why did she leave NOW? She looked forward to this even more than I did. It doesn't make any sense.*

"Excuse me?"

Ebony slipped out of her daze and looked up, only to meet the gaze of the two most beautiful brown eyes she had ever seen. They reminded her a lot of the eyes of her mother and sister, so that, for the split of a second, she thought Snow White had shown up for the ball after all.

But then she noticed that the skin around those eyes in front of her was tanned, much unlike the pale skin of her sister and framed by beautifully styled brown curls instead of ebony black hair.

"Yes, please?" Ebony heard herself say, even though she was still busy admiring the face in front of her.

Two perfectly curved lips started to smile and Ebony felt her lips return the gesture without even thinking about it.

"You must be lady Ebony, right?"

Ebony nodded, because she was lost for words. *If this is what love at first sight feels like, I understand why Snow White described it as magic. I just can't take my eyes off … who is this anyway?*

"It's a pleasure to meet you, lady Ebony. My name is princess Viola. I am from one of the kingdoms in the south. I'm not sure if your father ever mentioned this to you, but he visits our land on a regular basis. We have the most exquisite jewellery all around."

Ebony stared at the young woman in front of her and couldn't deny that her elegant necklace and earrings looked rather impressive.

"This one," Viola continued, "was made within my land, for example."

She pointed at the delicate necklace, which the king had given Ebony just for this occasion.

"Well," Ebony finally managed to say. "I have to admit that your people seem to be very skilled at what they do. Your jewellery is the most gorgeous and artistic that I've ever seen so far."

"Thank you," Viola beamed. "I once watched how they make those things. Seeing them do it is even more impressive than wearing these."

She pointed at her own necklace and laughed heartily.

"You – you watched them during their work?"

Ebony's eyes widened and her heart started to beat faster. *Could this really be? Am I not the only princess who cares about the work of the people?*

"Oh, yes," Viola raved enthusiastically. "I've watched them for a whole day. It was mind-blowing! Maybe your father can take you with him when he visits our kingdom again. I'd love to show you the jewellers!"

"I'd like that very much," Ebony breathed, while she felt her cheeks blush at the very thought of visiting Viola and spending a whole day within her presence. *Is this what love feels like?*

"That's decided then," Viola stated with a smile. "But let's return to the here and now. I don't know about the customs in your kingdom, but down in the south we dance at a ball."

"Um –"

"Would you like to dance with me?"

Ebony stared at Viola's outstretched hand, insecurity making it hard to breathe, while her heart was racing so fast that she thought it might explode.

"Me?"

"Sure," Viola giggled happily. "Why not? Aren't women allowed to dance with each other around here?"

"Well – It's just – unusual –"

"Who needs 'usual' if we can have fun? Those princes over there seem to be busy anyway. And I hate to miss a chance for a good dance – especially when the music is as nice as this."

With those words, Viola just took Ebony by the hand and dragged her towards the dance floor. She didn't seem to care about etiquette as much as the others and wasn't bothered by the other people who stared at them.

Ebony was used to being looked at with disapproval anyway and soon lost herself within the dance, not caring about tradition or decencies.

Viola was an excellent dancer and they glided over the polished marble as effortless as snowflakes gliding down from the heavens, the white feathers on Ebony's dress accentuating the image.

At times, Viola would lead with confident movements and then again change position, so that Ebony could lead her through the next dance.

Minutes turned into hours and hours into an eternity. Ebony completely lost track of time, while she whirled through the room, Viola's warm hand resting within hers. Viola's skin was soft and smooth, much like Snow White's, but her hair smelled of foreign flowers that Ebony didn't know. *Much more intriguing than the scent of roses. If Viola was a flower garden, I would spend all day in there, just like Snow White used to do around here.*

Most of the time, the two princesses would just enjoy the dancing without feeling the urge for conversation. Sometimes Viola would ask Ebony about the customs of her kingdom though and Ebony happily answered all her questions, thrilled that someone was fascinated by similar things than herself.

"Do you like horse-riding?" Viola inquired at one point and Ebony nodded.

"Oh, yes! I love my horse. Riding through the snowy landscape is wonderful – especially when the sun is out and everything is sparkling like a thousand diamonds."

"We don't really get much snow during the winter," Viola replied sadly. "But I can imagine that it must be beautiful over here. The feathers on your dress actually remind me a bit of dancing snowflakes. Maybe my father will allow us to visit one time, even though he always emphasises how dangerous it is to travel during winter."

"My father says the same," Ebony giggled. "He reminds me constantly that I shouldn't leave the castle grounds if the clouds look like they might bring fresh snow. It can get very cold during the winter and if you'd get lost during a snowstorm, you might freeze to death."

"Horrible." Viola shuddered. "Dying within the cold – the worst thing a southerner can imagine, I guess. In our land it's warm most of the time and we go riding for hours sometimes."

"Yes, we do, too, during the summer. Right now, it's nice for riding, for example. Just a few days ago, I was riding through the woods –"

Ebony broke off and stared into the depth of Viola's brown eyes. *Brown like Snow White's … I was riding through the forest – wasn't I? To find her maybe? Was I searching for Snow White? But why would she go into the woods? She hates getting dirty …*

"Is anything the matter?"

Viola's worried voice ripped Ebony out of her thoughts and brought her back to the ballroom.

"Huh? Oh – no. Sorry, I was just lost in thoughts –"

"You looked worried. Is it about your sister, Snow White? She is sick, right?"

"She – yes – well – My father doesn't want me to talk about it. But I am rather worried about her, yes."

Ebony eyed her dance partner with growing curiosity. *She is the first one who actually cares how I feel. All the others just want to know about Snow White and when they can see her. But Viola truly seems to care about MY feelings and thoughts.*

"It must be hard for you," Viola mused. "You two are twins, aren't you? I've once heard that twins actually have a bond between them. Sometimes they can even sense how the other one is feeling. Have you ever experienced anything like that?"

"No, I don't think so. You must know that Snow White and I are very different. She is all beautiful and everybody loves her. And I – well –"

"I think you are rather pretty."

Viola beamed at Ebony, who felt her cheeks blushing.

"You – you do?"

"Yes," Viola went on with honest admiration in her voice. "Your dark eyes remind me of a clear night sky. I love watching the sky turning black, just before the stars appear. Your eyes even sparkle a little like the stars. And your red hair – it's kind of mysterious. I've never seen someone with red hair actually! In the south, we all have brown or black hair. But yours is – it's different. In a good way. Special. Like a blooming rose."

"A rose?" Ebony arched her eyebrows. "That's funny. No one ever said anything like that to me before. The most common comparison is that of blood."

"Red like blood? Well, I guess it's fitting as well. But it definitely reminds me of the deep red shade of rose petals which are in full bloom. I always loved the dark red ones more than the light or pink ones."

"Me too!"

Now it was Ebony who beamed and Viola smiled in return. *We have so much in common – much more than Snow White and I ever had. Viola might as well be the kind of soulmate I always wanted. Can it be a coincidence that I just met her when my beloved big sister disappeared from my life?*

The ball went on deep into the night. At some point, the banquet was opened and people kept eating and dancing, until the moon shone into the room through the high windows.

Ebony would have loved to take Viola for a moonlight-walk within the castle gardens, but the guards wouldn't let her go outside.

"No one is to leave the castle after nightfall," one of the guards explained. "King's orders. I'm sorry, my lady."

"Too bad," Ebony sighed and turned towards Viola. "My father can be a bit overprotective sometimes. He worries about us more often since our mother died."

"Oh! I'm so sorry about that. I had heard about the tragedy, but totally forgot – my apologies."

"No, that's all right. It's been years since then. Even though I still miss her."

"I can only imagine how it must be to lose your mother. My mum and I are very close, even though I prefer to go horse-riding with my father. It must have been hard for all of you. Do you get along with the new queen though?"

"Not really," Ebony whispered. "I think she's rather cold and – I don't know. There is something weird about her."

"She's beautiful though," countered Viola and watched the queen, who was standing within a circle of admirers. "Not as beautiful as you, but –"

"Wait! You think that I'm more beautiful than *her?!*"

"Well, I guess it all depends on your perspective," Viola offered. "If you just take into account the looks, she might be more beautiful than you are. But there is something arrogant about her beauty. It seems superficial, like it doesn't match her character. But you … Your skin might be a bit too pale and your lips not as full as hers, but at least you have a magnetic personality. Your beauty shines from within, because you are good by nature and kind at heart."

"You think so?"

"Yes. My mother always says that I'm a good judge of character, so you can trust me when I say that your beauty is more natural and truer than that of the queen."

"Huh. And here I was, believing that no one even thought of me as pretty —"

"In that case, you are deeply mistaken!"

"Well, you haven't seen my sister yet," Ebony sighed, not able to suppress a hint of bitterness. "Normally people see the both of us together and neither the queen nor I could ever rival Snow White's beauty."

As soon as those words had left her mouth, a blurred memory flashed through Ebony's mind. The south tower. A secret chamber. The queen in front of a mirror, speaking to herself. *No, not herself! She was talking to the mirror! A magic mirror! But what were they saying?*

"Anyway," Viola exclaimed and brought Ebony back to the present. "Even though it might have been interesting to meet your sister, I'm glad that I got the chance to meet you today. It's funny — it feels like I've known you forever, even though it's just been one evening."

"The same goes for me," agreed Ebony and blushed again. "It's amazing how much we have in common. And I'm really looking forward to visiting your kingdom as soon as possible."

"And I'm looking forward to riding through the snow with you, whenever I get the chance to visit you during winter."

They smiled at each other, before Viola took Ebony by the hand and dragged her back towards the ballroom.

"We'd better not let our parents worry about our whereabouts. The ball will soon come to an end, I guess. Would you like to dance with me one last time?"

"Of course," Ebony replied without thinking and let herself be led onto the dance floor once more. *With you, I'd dance forever without ever getting bored or tired.*

The other ball guests didn't seem to share this opinion. Viola and Ebony managed to enjoy two more dances together, until the end of the ball was finally announced and everybody went to bed.

"Good night," Viola whispered when her mother came over to take her to their guest chamber. "And sweet dreams."

"The same to you," Ebony replied in a low voice, a joyful smile spreading over her face. *If I could dream of you, it would definitely be the sweetest dream I've ever had.*

At first, it seemed as if this wish of hers might actually come true. Ebony went to her chamber in a daze, reliving the memories of dancing with Viola and feeling her heart beat with excitement. It felt like it was pumping happiness through her veins instead of blood and her head was so light that she might as well have been floating.

When she lay down and closed her eyes, she could still see the beautiful face of Viola: her delicate nose, her big brown eyes, her high cheekbones, her tanned skin …

With a smile upon her face, Ebony dozed off and danced into the land of dreams, Viola in her arms and a clear night sky above their heads.

The silvery moonlight shone onto their faces, illuminating Viola's sparkling eyes and making her skin paler than it had been before. Ebony lost herself within the depth of her brown eyes, while they danced through the moonlight.

But then the dream started to change. The silvery light disappeared behind dark clouds, which soon covered the sky with a thick layer of dizzying gloom. Ebony looked up to see whether there was an end to the clouds, but it was too dark to make out clear shapes.

As she turned her gaze back towards Viola, she was gone. Instead, it was Snow White who was dancing with her through an empty ballroom. At first, she was laughing, but then she looked over Ebony's shoulder and went pale.

Ebony spun around to see what was bothering her sister, but there was nothing unusual to be seen. Just a curtain and behind it a closed wooden door.

Filled with confusion, Ebony turned around again, only to find that Snow White had disappeared as well.

"Snow White?" Ebony called out and fear started to grip her heart. "Where are you? Come back to me!"

"Follow me," whispered a distant voice which seemed to be coming from the wooden door.

"Snow White? Is that you?"

Ebony took a few steps towards the half-hidden door.

"Snow White?"

There was no answer anymore.

Ebony gathered all her courage and walked to the mysterious door. Her heart started to beat faster when she put her hand on the handle and slowly opened the door. When she peeked through the gap, she was surprised to find that there was a stone staircase behind it, leading upwards in spirals to a hidden end. *It looks like the queen's staircase within the south tower. But that is impossible!*

For a second, she hesitated, but her curiosity won out over her fear of the queen and she ventured on, slowly and quietly. The flight of steps seemed to be endless and Ebony lost track of time, until she suddenly reached another wooden door. This one was half open already and through the opening, she could see the queen walking towards her magic mirror. *The secret chamber! I'm in the south tower after all. But how is this possible?*

Ebony watched while the queen came to a halt in front of the mirror and looked into it with an arrogant smile upon her face.

"Mirror, mirror, on the wall, who is the fairest of us all?"

"You are the fairest for sure, my queen, because Snow White never again will be seen."

"Right you are. She's gone forever. But I heard someone call Ebony beautiful at the ball. Maybe we should get rid of her as well. I'll better call the huntsman –"

The huntsman!

Ebony woke up with a start, panting and gazing into the darkness with wide eyes. *There was a huntsman with me within the woods. What was his name again? Henry! Yes, that's it. But why did we go into the woods?*

She quickly tried to remember the other details of the dream, but they were starting to get blurred already and she couldn't get together what else she had seen.

For the rest of the night, she wasn't haunted by any such lively dreams anymore and when she woke up in the morning, only the distant memory remained, that there had been a huntsman named Henry, with whom she had ridden into the forest. *I should try to find this Henry and ask him about it. Maybe he can tell me why we rode off in the first place …*

To Ebony's great disappointment, there was no huntsman named Henry to be found within the castle. As she went to the sleeping charters of the huntsmen, no one was there and she remembered that her father had sent them all into the nearby villages, searching for a sign of Snow White.

When she asked the servants and guards about a huntsman named Henry, they could only tell her that there once had been a man with that name, but he had disappeared a few days ago and nobody knew where he went to.

"This is stupid," Ebony mumbled to herself with frustration welling up inside her when she got back to her room. "Why can't I remember anything about the day that Snow White disappeared? I've got to concentrate!"

The latter wasn't exactly made easier by the fact that there was to be another ball in the evening. Most of the guests had come from afar and didn't want to leave after just one day, so the king had organised a banquet at midday and another ball for the night.

Ebony was looking forward to seeing Viola again, but the butterflies in her stomach weren't helping her to remember. In fact, they weren't helpful with anything at all. They even made her lose her appetite and she was actually playing with the thought of skipping the banquet, but she also longed to speak to Viola again. *She seemed to understand me. Maybe I could find a way to speak to her in private and tell her about Snow White's disappearance. It might be easier to solve this mystery together.*

When she reached the great dining hall though, Ebony instantly knew that it would be difficult to leave without being noticed by the adults.

The princes and princesses had been seated close to the high windows and anyone who entered or left the room had to pass the table of the kings and queens – not to mention all the servants, who were keeping a close eye on Ebony since she had vanished into the woods herself.

At least there was one bright spot to be found: The seat to Viola's right was still empty and Ebony was greeted by a radiant smile when she sat down at the table beside her new friend.

"Good day, lady Ebony. It's great to see you again."

"The same goes for seeing you, lady Viola," Ebony breathed, her jubilating heart making it difficult to speak. "But please, just call me Ebony."

"All right. But only if you call me Viola."

"Agreed."

"Wonderful!" Viola gave Ebony a charming smile and made Ebony's heart pick up its speed even more. "I hope you slept well last night?"

"Um …"

Ebony looked around at all the others, who seemed to be busy with their own conversations. *But they might still be listening. It's not safe to talk openly around so many nosy ears.*

"It was not too bad," Ebony replied evasively and helped herself to some food. "What about you?"

"Oh, I never sleep well when I'm away from home. At least not for the first few nights. But I was able to watch the stars from our window. They were beautiful! It actually reminded me of your eyes."

Viola gazed openly into Ebony's surprised face and made her blush, completely forgetting about her food for a few minutes.

"I thought of you as well," Ebony whispered. "You even visited my dreams." *Did I really just say that out loud?!*

"Wow! You flatter me, Ebony."

Viola beamed at her, while her cheeks gained a little more colour. *Now I'm not the only one blushing anymore.* Ebony returned the smile, her heart beating even faster.

Only when Viola turned back towards her plate, Ebony finally remembered her food, too, and started to eat again. The butterflies within her stomach made this a difficult task and she soon stopped eating, being too filled by joyous feelings.

"Would you like to go for a walk?" Viola asked when she had finished her lunch. "I'm sure you'll be allowed to show me the castle gardens during the day, right?"

"I'd love to." *I just hope that nobody will object if we try to leave …*

They both got up and left the grand hall, not being stopped by their parents or the servants. Ebony noticed that the castle guards on the walls kept a close eye on them though, as if to make sure that they wouldn't run off. *Is this because of Snow White? Or because I went to the woods?*

"You have beautiful flowers here," Viola exclaimed as they reached one of Snow White's favourite spots of the garden.

Ebony just nodded and watched Viola, while they walked among the pleasant sight of roses, lilies, sunflowers, petunias and other blooms.

"This one looks like your hair!" Viola pointed towards a dark red rose with lush petals. "Dark and beautiful. Very fitting for you."

Ebony blushed – *Is this ever going to stop again!?* – while she followed Viola further through the garden. When she was sure that no one was close enough to listen to their conversation, she took a deep breath and turned towards Viola with an earnest look.

"You know – there – there is something that I didn't want to mention earlier when you asked me about last night. That is to say, I didn't want to talk about the not so pleasant dreams that I had."

"Did you have a nightmare?" Viola asked with concern, while she stopped to admire the flowers and looked at Ebony instead.

"Yes, something like that," Ebony mumbled, not sure how to tell Viola the truth. "It was a very dark dream. My sister was there – but then she vanished. And there was this wooden door. It let to – to the – That doesn't really matter. But I think it had something to do with the disappearance of my sister. There was this huntsman – or at least he was mentioned by the queen –"

"Wait!" Viola exclaimed and locked shocked. "Your sister is gone?"

"Oh, right," Ebony remembered. "You wouldn't know about that. Yes, that's another thing that I couldn't tell you earlier. My father wants to keep it a secret, because he doesn't want the other queens and kings to worry about the safety of their children."

"Your sister isn't sick then? She ran away?"

"Well, we don't exactly know that. But she has been gone for days and nobody has seen her. The guards didn't see her leave, but she could have slipped out one of the exits at the back. They're not as heavily guarded as the main gate. At least they weren't before Snow White disappeared. Now this place turned into a fortress –"

"Do you mean that she didn't tell anyone where she was going to? Not even you?"

"That's right," Ebony sighed sadly. "She didn't mention that she was planning to go anywhere. I mean, why would she? There was nothing out there for her. And she was looking forward to this ball so much! I don't understand why she would miss it. It's not very like her."

"Do you think she was kidnapped?" Viola asked Ebony with wide eyes.

"I don't know," Ebony admitted. "But there is something strange about it all. And this dream about the huntsman – there was more, but I forgot the details –"

"And now you think that the huntsman might have something to do with all that?"

"Maybe. I'm sure that there is a connection. I just can't see it. My head feels dizzy whenever I try to think of it. Just as if something inside me doesn't want to remember."

"Mysterious."

"Yes, far too mysterious for my liking. I'd rather see the clear picture and find out where Snow White might be. I don't want to lose her – not like my mother –"

"I understand." Viola took Ebony's hand into hers and caressed it with gentle fingers. "Is there anything I can do to help you?"

Ebony stared at Viola for a few seconds, not sure what to think or feel. The mere touch of Viola's fingers made her heart go crazy and she noticed that she was actually holding her breath.

But then the image of Snow White appeared before her mind's eye and reminded her of the more urgent matters.

"I'm not sure. I don't really know where to start –"

"Let's look at what you already know for sure," Viola suggested calmly. "How long has your sister been gone?"

"Today is the sixth day, including the one she vanished."

"All right. And no one saw her leave?"

"Not a soul."

"Do you know where she was last seen?"

"Right within these gardens." Ebony gave the roses a wistful look and could almost hear Snow White's clear voice dancing through the air. "She loved to play among the flowers. It was her favourite place within the castle grounds."

"Is there some kind of exit around here? Maybe even a secret passage?"

"Not that I would know of."

"Let's have a look around the walls."

Viola pulled Ebony towards the high stone walls and they walked along them, while they collected more facts and details about Snow White's disappearance.

"There was no trace of her within or around the castle?"

"None at all," replied Ebony with a sigh. "I searched the whole castle myself and my father has been sending his men to all villages close by. I think I even went into the forest to look for her – but I can't really remember –"

"Why would she go into the forest?"

"No idea. That's what bothers me. I just can't think of a reason for her to go there, but that's where I went – with the huntsman, I think."

"So there really was a huntsman?"

"Yes. His name was Henry, but no one has seen him ever since. It's like he vanished, just like Snow White did."

"Maybe there is some kind of monster within the forest which holds them prisoner," whispered Viola, while she let her fingertips glide over the stonewall. "Or an evil witch who turned them into trees!"

Ebony stopped.

"An evil witch," she murmured, her eyes going blank. "Yes, that might actually be close to the truth."

Viola eyed her with scepticism.

"It was actually meant as a joke —"

"But what if it's true? There is something within me that's telling me witchcraft might be involved in some way. If only I could remember! Give me a second."

Ebony stared into oblivion while she desperately tried to clear her mind, which was starting to feel rather dizzy and clouded again. *A witch — an evil witch. I think I saw a witch — or at least something magical — magical — Yes! The magic mirror, up in the south tower. The queen might be a witch. But how would she have made Snow White and the huntsman disappear? Could the mirror do such a thing?*

"Any ideas yet?" Viola asked with curiosity in her brown eyes. "Do you really think that it was a witch?"

"Maybe. I'm not sure about the details yet. But I think we're getting closer."

"We are indeed. Look!" Viola uncovered a hidden door which was completely overgrown with tendrils of vine. "Maybe your sister went through here."

"Well, even if she did, I'm afraid we can't."

Ebony looked up towards the top of the stonewall. One of the guards was keeping an eye on them as if he was suspecting them to vanish right before his eyes.

"I wonder where it leads to," mused Viola. "Do you think we could at least take a look?"

"We can try," agreed Ebony and searched for a doorhandle under the green leaves.

"Oi," the guard called down with a nervous voice. "What are you two ladies up to?"

Ebony stepped back from the stone wall and looked up into the stern face of the guard.

"We just wanted to know where this secret door leads to. Could you tell us?"

"Secret door?" The guard furrowed his brows. "What are you talking about? Which door? And where?"

"Right here, within the wall below your feet," replied Ebony and pointed towards the tendrils of vine. "Have you never noticed it?"

"If this is a trick to make me leave my post, it won't work. I was ordered to keep watch *on the wall* and that's where I'll stay."

"We don't want to trick you," Ebony ensured him with honesty in her voice. "You can stay up there if you want to. But please let us have a look at this door to see where it leads to."

The guard didn't seem to be very happy about this request, but nodded after a few thoughtful seconds.

"All right. But one of you has to stay behind. And if you don't answer my calls anymore, I'll send someone down to look for you. So don't even try to run away!"

"Of course," Ebony answered and turned back to Viola. "Why does everybody think that I would like to run away as well? If that's what Snow White did anyway —"

"I guess, they are just worried," countered Viola and tried to free the door from the tendrils of vine. "Look! There's the handle."

They both looked at each other with excitement in their eyes. Then Viola pushed down the handle and Ebony's heart started to race, while they both pulled the heavy door open.

"Well, well," Viola exclaimed. "What have we here?! If that's not a secret passageway, I'm not a princess!"

Ebony nodded, the blood rushing through her veins.

"I wonder where it leads to," she whispered and held her breath as she took a step forward to gaze into the darkness behind the door.

"Remember," the guard called down with panic in his voice. "One of you stays behind! And you have to stay within earshot or I'll —"

"— send someone down," Ebony shouted up. "Yes, we know. I won't go far, I promise."

She took another step and gazed into the dark tunnel. There was no light to be seen, so she guessed that it was either very long or bent around a few corners and thus blocked out the light at its end.

"Can you see anything?" Viola asked, while she tried to peek into the tunnel herself, while staying within the viewing range of the guard.

"Not really," Ebony answered with disappointment in her voice. "I can't make out a light at the end. Maybe the exit is blocked. But it's definitely a passage and there are stones on the ground. Seems like it was built as some kind of secret escape route."

"Well, there's no way of finding out where it leads to if we can't go in. Maybe we can ask your father. He should know about this. It's his castle after all."

"Yes, I guess, we could give it a try."

Ebony gazed into the tunnel for a few more seconds, trying to make out any footprints or other proof that her sister might have used this passage. There was nothing of the sort though and she finally gave up.

Together with Viola, she shut the heavy door again and then went back into the castle, hoping that the banquet was over and they would get a chance to talk to her father alone.

They found the king deep in conversation with a few of the lords who had attended the ball as well. Not wanting to disturb them, Ebony and Viola retreated into the library instead and passed the time by reading their favourite passages out of several books to each other.

Ebony was thrilled to find out that Viola loved reading just as much as she did, even though their preferences weren't exactly the same when it came to the choice of genre.

"I love ghost stories and tales about magic," Viola stated, while she pulled one of said books out of the shelf and started to flip through the pages.

"I prefer adventurous stories with strong heroes," countered Ebony. "Ghost stories are too fictional for my taste. I don't believe in ghosts in the first place, so why would I want to read about them?"

"Well, why would you want to read about adventures instead of having them?" replied Viola and grinned. "Isn't it more fascinating to imagine what could exist – like ghosts or fairies – instead of concentrating on the things we already know to be there?"

"You actually believe in ghosts and fairies then?"

"Yes. Why not? I'm sure that there are a lot of things which we can't see with our eyes – like air or magic, for example. So why not ghosts?"

"I don't know. It just never seemed very likely to me."

"But you believe in witches, don't you? You said that there might be witchcraft involved –"

"Shush!"

Ebony put a finger over her mouth and quickly glanced over her shoulder to see whether there was anyone else within the library.

"It's best not to talk about this in here," she whispered and put back the novel she had just been reading from. "We should go back to my father and see if he has time for us now."

"All right."

Viola put back her book and followed Ebony through the hallways, which were filled by busy servants and conversing guests, who were on their way into the gardens.

The king on the other hand was to be found within the throne room, this time in the company of one of the huntsmen, who had returned from one of the villages and was giving his report.

"No sign of Snow White whatsoever," he was just saying as Ebony and Viola entered the room.

The king sighed, but then forced a smile onto his face as he turned to greet the two girls.

"Ebony, my dear. What are you doing inside? It's a beautiful day! You might show lady Viola our gardens –"

"We've already been there," Ebony blurted out. "And we – that is, lady Viola – found a secret passageway. It was hidden behind a thick wooden door, which was all covered by tendrils of vine. I never noticed it before, but maybe Snow White did. She always used to spend so much time within the gardens! What if she went through there? Do you know where it leads to?"

She stopped and looked at her father with eager eyes.

The king had furrowed his brows and seemed to be thinking hard. Then he turned towards the huntsman, who was still with them.

"Send some men down there. Let them search the passageway and look for footprints at the exit. Maybe Ebony is right. Snow White might have found the passageway and gotten lost within the forest."

"Yes, your highness."

The huntsman turned around and hurried off, while Ebony stared at her father with wide eyes.

"It leads towards the forest then?" she whispered.

"It ends right at the edge of the forest, yes," answered the king and then gazed at Viola with a nervous look. "Did you, by any chance, tell lady Viola here about Snow White's disappearance?"

"Um – well – I might have mentioned it –"

"Didn't I tell you *not* to talk about it?"

"Yes, you did, father," Ebony admitted ruefully. "But I just couldn't keep it a secret any longer. And Viola won't tell anybody! She just wanted to help – and she did. Without her, I never would have found that hidden door."

"I see."

The king eyed the two young women, who were darting a nervous side glance at each other. *I just hope that I didn't get Viola into trouble now. Maybe I shouldn't have let my father know what I told her.*

"Well," the king finally continued with a heavy sigh. "What's done, is done. I just hope that you two can keep this a secret from now on. I wouldn't want any of my guests to worry about their safety."

"Of course," Ebony and Viola answered simultaneously. "We won't tell anyone!"

"Good."

"But why would Snow White go into the forest?" Ebony mused and looked at her father with a puzzled look. "She doesn't even like the woods. She prefers fields of flowers and would never leave the castle without permission."

"I really don't know," answered the king with a grave voice. "I've been wondering about that myself ever since I came back. Of the two of you, *you* are the curious and adventurous one for sure."

"True," Ebony agreed. "It just doesn't make any sense."

"If I may be so bold," Viola joined the conversation with polite curiosity on her face. "May I ask whether lady Snow White might have had a secret lover?"

Both the king and Ebony stared at Viola with wide eyes.

"I don't think so," the king then said with emphasis. "She never mentioned anyone."

"Well, she wouldn't, would she?" Ebony grinned. "It is called *secret* lover for a reason."

"Yes, but she never met men outside the castle grounds," the king argued. "Only at balls. And even there she never seemed to fall in love with anyone. Right?"

He turned towards Ebony with a pleading look.

"Yes, I think you're right. She actually mentioned to me that she wished to meet her 'love at first sight' at this ball, so I don't think that she ever loved anyone before."

"Just a thought," Viola replied and blushed a little.

"Well, thank you for your help," the king said to her with a kind smile. "But now you two should really go out into the garden and enjoy the lovely sunshine. I'll let you know if we find any new leads."

Ebony and Viola nodded and went out of the throne room, both lost within their own thoughts. *If the passageway leads into the forest, it would make sense that I went there, too, to look for her. But how did I find out about this? I'm sure that I've never seen that secret door before. Did this Henry know about it? Did he lead me into the forest to show me where Snow White went? But what happened to the both of them? Where are they? And why can't I remember?*

113

While Ebony and Viola spent the rest of the day in the garden, hoping to see Snow White stumbling out of the secret passageway, they were not only watched by the nervous castle guards.

Far above their heads, up in the Cloud Castle, the young fairy apprentice was giving the old Good Fairy a hard time as well.

"We should intervene," she was arguing with emphasis, flying hither and thither within the Chamber of Sight, from which the two had been watching Ebony with Viola. "This can't go on any longer. We've got to help them find Snow White and bring the new queen to justice!"

"Absolutely not," exclaimed the Good Fairy. "We fairies don't intervene and we certainly do not decide what is just and what isn't. That's not how the world works. The humans have got to solve this on their own."

"But we can't just let the queen get away with it!"

"Just because she's not imprisoned yet, doesn't mean that she won't be hold responsible for her actions. Every act of evil – and of kindness, too – has its consequences."

"But when?" whined the young fairy impatiently. "When will there be consequences?"

"Sometimes it takes a while until the true outcome of a situation reveals itself. You've got to be patient. Every evil deed is judged in the end."

"But who's judging it, if we can't intervene?"

"Life itself is the most just judge of all," the Good Fairy stated wisely. "Even if we might think that things are not going well or that something is unfair, life will eventually set it right again. You only have to be patient and believe in the inescapability of truth."

"You mean the queen will be punished for her evil actions? Will she be thrown into the dungeons? Or banned from the kingdom?"

"I don't know. I won't look into the future, because I have faith in life and justice. Every wrong can be made right again. But that is life's duty – not ours."

"If you say so."

The young fairy gazed at the mirror, which showed Snow White happily dancing through the garden of the seven dwarves. Then, with a heavy sigh, she turned back towards the mirror showing Ebony and Viola, who were still sitting in the garden and waiting for any news to arrive from the forest.

"You know," the Good Fairy muttered, "I'm not sure if you really paid attention when you were preparing the magic potion for princess Ebony."

"Why not? She turned out rather witty and even pretty, don't you think?"

"I wasn't talking about looks. It's obvious that she should eat more and get those female curves into shape. Her bosom is small and her arms look skinny –"

"I thought you didn't want to talk about her looks," Arabella interrupted her with a sulky face. "You don't have to start with it just to insult her."

"Well, I didn't intend to. I was actually more worried about her love interest. She seems to be far too interested in women for my taste."

"Huh? Is there anything wrong with that?"

"Society isn't ready for women who fall in love with each other. It's just not normal!"

"Who needs normal?" grumbled the young fairy. "Normal is boring! And who decides what is normal and what isn't? Why not open your mind for new ideas? I think she and Viola are a beautiful couple! They are both curious and caring and –"

"– women! They are women." The Good Fairy looked distressed. "Don't you see that this could be a problem? Ebony is a princess after all. And if Snow White shouldn't return to the castle –"

"But I thought that this matter would solve itself in the end? Didn't you say that everything was going to be fine?"

"Not exactly. I said that every wrong can be turned into a right. It doesn't have to mean that Snow White will return to her father though."

"But – but then – Ebony would be –"

"Exactly! The future queen and ruler of this kingdom," the Good Fairy sighed, sounding on edge. "And that's why she just *can't* fall in love with a woman. It's unheard of! A queen who loves women? How would she get an heir?"

"Does she have to have an heir?" Arabella asked puzzled. "Couldn't she just name some suitable successor? Or let the people decide whom they want as the next ruler?"

"The people?" The Good Fairy laughed out loud. "Don't be silly. Since when do *the people* decide what's best for them? There is always an elite of privileged ones who rule over all the others. What kind of world would that be if everyone had a say in every matter? Maybe even equal rights for everyone?"

"What's so bad about that?"

"Ha! That would be anarchy!"

"No, it wouldn't have to be," the young fairy protested emphatically. "It might be a democratic community in which everyone is important and valued. Why would there have to be an elite of people who get all the privileges, all the power, all the wealth and money? That's just not fair!"

116

"Enough of that!" The Good Fairy gave her apprentice a stern look. "This nonsense has to be stopped."

"I thought we shouldn't intervene –?"

"We won't. But I'll keep an eye on that lady Viola. It would only raise more problems if your Ebony grows too fond of her."

"But they are in love!" Arabella exclaimed with a dreamy look in her blue eyes. "Isn't that beautiful? I'm definitely happy for them."

"Well, you shouldn't be. Their love won't be accepted and thus would only cause trouble and pain. You'd better hope that it's merely a fling."

"I think it's true love," insisted the young fairy and pulled a sulky face while she left the Chamber of Sight alongside her mistress. "And true love is always stronger than the suspicion of anyone around it."

"I hope for you that this is true," sighed the Good Fairy and led her apprentice back into the main hall. "But now let us concentrate on your education again. Which are the main principles of being a good fairy?"

𝕰𝖛𝖊𝖓𝖎𝖓𝖌 came and crushed Ebony's hope of finally finding a sign of Snow White. The huntsman and his men returned from their search empty-handed and told the king that there were no traces whatsoever at the end of the secret passageway.

"There were signs of fresh dirt within the tunnel," the huntsman reported. "But no footprints could be found at the edge of the forest. If there ever was any proof that your daughter went through there, it's gone by now."

The king sighed and thanked his men for their efforts, until he sent them away and turned to Ebony instead. Viola had already been summoned by her parents to get ready for the second night of the ball.

Ebony had been looking forward to dancing with Viola again, but now she had lost all of her desire to attend to the ball at all.

"I'm sorry, my dear," said the king and looked at her with tired eyes. "There is nothing more we can do right now. You should go to your room and get ready for the ball. It's getting late already and we wouldn't want to let our guests wait, would we?"

"I'm not really in the mood for festivities right now," mumbled Ebony. "Couldn't you pretend that I have fallen sick as well?"

"Oh, my dear. What would the guests think if my second daughter misses the ball too? They might get worried that we've been afflicted with some kind of plague. And you promised lady Viola to dance with her again, didn't you?"

Ebony sighed and nodded.

"I did."

"Well, you'd better not keep her waiting then." The king tried to smile encouragingly. "I'm glad that you finally found a friend – apart from your sister, I mean."

"Yes. I'm glad too." *Even though I hope that she might actually be more than just a friend.*

Ebony returned the smile without much enthusiasm and went to her room to get dressed for the ball.

Viola was already waiting for her within the ballroom when Ebony finally showed up. The music was playing and most of the guests were dancing, except Viola, who waited close to the doors.

"There you are," she greeted Ebony with glinting eyes. "Any news from – well – you know –?"

"Not really," whispered Ebony and let herself be pulled towards the dance floor. "There were no signs or traces within the forest. Only fresh dirt within the passageway. But that's all."

"Well, that's something, isn't it? At least you now know where lady Sno– I mean – where *she* went. Maybe that will help you to track her down."

"Yes. Hopefully."

The music stopped for a few seconds and Viola took Ebony's hand to join in the next dance. Ebony just let it happen and tried to rid her mind of her worries for a few hours to enjoy Viola's company.

Fortunately, it was rather easy to get lost within Viola's deep brown eyes and joyful smile. At some part, Ebony lost track of time and managed to forget about Snow White for a while, even though the chocolates from the banquet reminded her of her elder sister a lot. *She always loved the ones with white chocolate, while I preferred the dark ones. I wonder which Viola's favourites might be?*

While her eyes stayed on Viola most of the time, she noticed that some of the other guests were eyeing them from time to time, while they glided gracefully over the polished marble floor.

At first, she ignored their frowns and furrowed brows, but when two foreign queens started to whisper on the quiet, she couldn't help wondering whether they had noticed how much Ebony cared about her new friend. *It probably wouldn't be wise to let everyone know about my feelings for Viola. Maybe I should dance with a few of the princes, too, just to keep the suspicions at bay.*

She was about to tell Viola about this plan, when she overheard a whispered conversation of a prince and a princess who were dancing nearby.

"– totally weird!"

"I always thought that lady Ebony was a bit 'different', but this is really awkward. They've been dancing with each other for an hour now!"

"I wonder what their parents think about this."

Ebony flinched and shot a glance at her father. He was dancing with one of the foreign queens and looked worried, even though he was clearly trying to hide his distress behind a polite smile. *Is he worried about Snow White or because his younger daughter is in love with a woman?*

"Is something the matter?"

Viola's concerned voice brought Ebony back to her dance partner and another pair of worried eyes. *Seems like I'm really good at worrying people.*

"No," Ebony answered evasively. "Not really. I was just thinking – Isn't it the duty of the host's daughter to dance with most of the princes?"

"I don't know about your kingdom, but in the south we just dance with pretty much every guest in the room. The gender doesn't really matter that much."

Ebony was tempted to ask whether the gender didn't matter as well when it came to relationships, but she couldn't make herself speak about her feelings for Viola.

"Well, around here it does matter," she replied instead and eyed the guests around them. "And I think that I've been very bad at fulfilling that duty so far."

"Oh!" Viola grinned. "I'm sorry. I didn't mean to keep you to myself. It's just very nice to dance and talk with you. I've never had a friend with whom I connected so quickly."

Ebony blushed a little and returned the grin.

"Thank you. I like spending time with you too."

"No harm done then?"

"None at all."

"Wonderful!"

Viola beamed at Ebony and ended their dance with a graceful turn, at the end of which they were suddenly much closer to each other than before.

"I really like you *a lot*," Viola whispered, before she took a step back and made a curtsy.

Ebony's cheeks started to burn while she returned the curtsy with a joyful smile. Before she could overcome her happy speechlessness though, their moment was ended by a quiet cough beside them.

"Hrumph, hrumph."

Both Ebony and Viola turned around to meet the gaze of a tall and dark-haired prince, who was eyeing them with a smirk.

"Sorry to bother you, ladies. I was wondering if I might have the honour of dancing with lady Viola?"

"Of course." Viola smiled and offered her hand to the tall prince. "I'd be delighted."

The two swept away from Ebony, but not before Viola had given her another ravishing smile, which made Ebony's heart beat faster. *She really likes me! A lot! Could that mean that she loves me too? If this is what love feels like anyway ...*

She watched while Viola glided over the dance floor with the dark-haired prince and only noticed after a few seconds that she was still standing within the middle of the marble floor.

Avoiding collision with other dancing couples, Ebony quickly slipped off the dance floor – only to find herself right beside her father who had quit dancing as well.

"Looks like you have been enjoying the evening so far," the king mused while he, too, watched Viola moving gracefully around the hall.

"Well, it was a nice change to being worried about – you know what –"

"Yes, I understand. But wouldn't you like to distract yourself a little more? With one or two charming princes perhaps?"

"Viola told me that they dance with everyone at the balls in the south. But I'm not sure if I could endure that. My feet are already starting to ache –"

"You don't have to keep up with your southern friend," the king replied smiling. "But there are a few princes who have been eyeing you all evening. I'm sure they wouldn't mind getting a chance to know you better."

"Right," Ebony snorted quietly. "As if anyone is really interested in *me*."

"What's that supposed to mean?" the king asked with a worried frown.

"It means that, the last time I danced with a prince, he only asked questions about Snow White. And when he noticed that I wouldn't give away anything about her, he was gone very quickly."

"But that doesn't have to mean that no one is interested in you, my dear. You should give the male dancing partners another chance. For my sake."

Ebony looked at her father and tried to see within his eyes whether he was actually against her relationship with Viola. The concern in his eyes reminded her that he was probably worrying about getting her married soon enough to ensure that their bloodline would have an heir.

The new queen doesn't seem to be able to bear children, so he won't get the son he always wanted. If Snow White doesn't show up again, I'll be his only hope. Then he'll never accept my feelings for Viola! I have to find my sister and make sure that she inherits the throne so that no one would mind if I don't produce an heir. I wonder why the new queen won't bear any children?

"As you wish, father."

Ebony tried her best to smile and turned towards the few princes who were not occupied on the dance floor. One of them caught her gaze and soon enough, she was gliding over the marble floor again, led by a young man named Richard, who's green eyes reminded her of the depth of the forest. *Snow White should better be alive and healthy. Next time I ride into the woods, I'll make sure to find her and bring her back so that father can get busy marrying her instead of me.*

The next morning brought with it aching feet and the pain of goodbye. Just like the rest of the guests, Viola and her parents were going to travel back to their kingdom right after breakfast.

Ebony had hoped to be able to talk to Viola in private before they had to part, but luck was not on their side. The both of them were watched by their parents at all times and barely had a chance to talk to each other during breakfast. Ebony's father kept reminding her that it was her duty to say goodbye to all the guests and thus she was rather busy with everything but her own concerns and feelings.

When it was the turn of Viola's family to part from them, Ebony could feel her heart pounding furiously against her chest as if it was protesting against letting her loved one go. *We've only just met! Why do we have to part so soon?*

Viola's eyes seemed to ask the same question while they exchanged formal words of parting. When their parents were busy talking to each other though, Viola secretly took a step forward and whispered very lowly:

"I'm going to miss you, Ebony. I'll think of you every night as I watch the starlit sky. It will remind me of the most beautiful eyes I've ever seen."

Ebony blushed slightly and took a step forward as well, so that their parents wouldn't hear her quiet answer.

"I'll miss you, too, Viola. But I truly hope that we'll be able to see each other again soon. And then we can spend a whole day together, while you show me the artful craft of making the most beautiful jewellery in the world." She pointed to her own necklace. "Until then, I'll wear this every day and think of your sparkling eyes and radiant smile, which have enchanted my heart."

Viola beamed at her and was about to reply something, but then their parents stopped talking and the two princesses quickly stepped apart. Ebony could feel a sting in her heart while she watched Viola leave and swore to herself that they would see each other again as soon as possible.

Her father on the other hand seemed to have other plans for her. He encouraged her to talk to every prince who said his goodbyes and even granted her some extra time when he thought that the conversation sounded promising.

Ebony longed to flee to her chambers, but time was merciless and stretched out for what seemed to be an eternity.

A lot of "safe travels" and "thank you for coming" later, Ebony had finally delt with the last prince and was allowed to retreat to her room before lunch.

The walls of the castle seemed suffocating and cold to her though and thus she went into the garden instead, walking along the path which she had shown to Viola only one day ago. *I just hope that father will let me visit her. He seemed very determined to match me with one of those princes.*

Her eyes fell upon the blooming petals of a white rose and the face of her sister flashed through her memory, making her heart ache even more. *All women whom I love seem to get taken from me. First my mother, gone forever. Then Snow White, lost in the woods. And now Viola. Who knows when we'll see each other again? Maybe she'll even forget me if it takes too long …*

Ebony sighed and lay back on the grass, staring into the sky with blank eyes, while her thoughts travelled in circles. Memories of Viola and Snow White started to blend and made her feel lost and lonely.

This feeling didn't leave her during lunch, even though her attention was soon attracted by the queen, who seemed to be in an unusually joyful mood.

"That was a splendid ball, my dearest," she crooned into the king's ear and fluttered her eyelashes. "We should have balls like that more often!"

"Of course, my love," the king replied with a gentle smile. "But first we've got to find Snow White. As soon as she's back, we'll have all the reasons in the world to have a ball every month."

The queen didn't look like she agreed to that, but she said nothing and left the king in his belief that she actually cared about his loss.

Ebony saw through her false charade though, because her vision was not blurred by feelings of love. She eyed the queen with suspicion and wondered whether she was truly involved in the disappearance of Snow White. But as soon as she tried to concentrate on the topic, her mind was clouded by distracting thoughts, which kept her from thinking straight.

𝖂𝖍𝖎𝖑𝖊 the foreign kings and queens left the castle and the kingdom, the Good Fairy watched Ebony and the king from her Chamber of Sight. The young fairy apprentice was there, too, but rather interested in Viola's journey, trying to find out whether the princess might actually have true feelings for Ebony.

"They're better off without each other," stated the Good Fairy with a satisfied smile and turned to leave the chamber. "I think I'll leave you in charge for a few days and go on a journey myself. You should be fine without me. But no rash decisions and granted wishes this time!"

"I shall try my best," Arabella replied. "May I ask where you're going?"

"I'll tell you when I get back. Just make sure that the kingdom doesn't turn into a mess while I'm away."

"Oh. You're going to leave the kingdom?"

"Yes. But don't worry. I'll be back soon enough."

With that and a glance at the mirror showing lady Viola with her parents, the Good Fairy left the chamber.

The young fairy followed her quickly to see in which direction her mistress would take off. She was a little worried that the Good Fairy might mess with Viola's feelings to ensure that she wouldn't fall in love with Ebony and sure enough, the old fairy left the Cloud Castle at the exit towards the south.

"I just hope that she stays true to her own rules and doesn't intervene," the young fairy mumbled.

Then an idea struck her mind and sparked hope within her heart. With the carefree determination of youth, the young fairy flew down towards the castle on the ground as fast as she could. She knew where to find Ebony and hid among the rose bushes to watch the red-haired princess walk through the garden. It was already getting dark and the fairy spotted a servant walking towards them.

"Damn it," she whispered and crawled back deeper into the rose bush.

"Lady Ebony," the servant called out from the marble steps. "It's time for dinner, my lady. You should come inside now before you catch a cold."

"It's far too warm to get cold out here," replied Ebony, but followed the servant inside the castle, crushing the young fairy's plans.

But she wasn't willing to give up that easily. She flew back to the Cloud Castle and watched Ebony through one of the mirrors in the Chamber of Sight.

As soon as dinner was over, the princess retreated into her own room. The young fairy waited until Ebony had lain down on her bed and closed her eyes. Then she flew back to the castle and silently entered the chamber of the sleeping princess.

"She looks beautiful in her sleep," the young fairy whispered to herself, while she approached the princess, hovering in the air just above the pillow.

Then, with a gentle shake of her wings, she let a little bit of fairy dust rain down from her wings and hair. It glided down like tiny snowflakes and landed upon the face of the sleeping princess.

"May your mind be as sharp as it was before and your memory return to you in full detail so that you can find those whom you love the most and bring them back into your life as long as they're still within this world."

The young fairy put a bit of magic into her words of blessing and let another glittery bit of fairy dust rain down onto Ebony's white skin. Then she left the chamber as silently as she had entered it and flew back to the Cloud Castle to watch how her little scheme would play out.

The Good Fairy had not yet returned and thus the young fairy made sure to keep an eye on the whole kingdom, while Ebony was lost in the land of dreams and not yet knew what awaited her when she would wake up.

𝕲𝖗𝖊𝖞 mist clouded her vision, while Ebony ran through a dark forest filled with fog and creepy sounds. She knew that she was dreaming, but she couldn't make herself leave the forest, even though she ran as fast as she could. There seemed to be no end to the trees and bushes. Her legs were tired and her feet aching.

When she looked down, she noticed that the ground was covered in snow and ice. Its perfect whiteness was only disturbed by her footprints, which were dark red from the blood of her naked feet.

She stopped and stared at the blood with tired eyes. *White as snow and red as blood. And there are ebony trees within these woods too. So why isn't my sister? It would be the perfect hiding place for her.*

With a heavy sigh, she started to walk again. As she lifted her gaze, she noticed that the fog was retreating and clearing her vision. Hope sparked within her heart and made her feet go faster, until she spotted a faint light in the distance.

Ebony gathered all her strength and ran towards the light with long strides. It got brighter as she approached it and all of a sudden, she reached the edge of the dark forest. She had to cover her eyes, so bright was the light outside the woods. It blinded her at first, but then her eyes got used to it and she could make out a path which led towards her father's castle.

As she started to walk along this path though, she noticed that its stones were covered in bits of broken glass, which sparkled like fresh snow in the sunlight. It cut open her naked feet even further and slowed her down, leaving a bloody trail wherever she stepped.

Ebony gritted her teeth and walked on, until she reached the castle and stepped through the open gates. Even there, within the castle grounds, there was a trail of shattered glass and she followed it bravely, even though the pain in her feet was killing her.

As she reached the queen's chamber, she noticed that there was blood on the threshold, covering the glass fragments before the door. Her heart picked up its pace while she sneaked into the chamber and up the stone staircase, leaving a trail of blood of her own.

When she reached the top of the tower and peeked into the secret chamber, she saw the queen standing in front of her magic mirror. Its glass was shattered and covered the ground, while the queen stood in the midst of the glass fragments. In her hand she was holding what looked like a chunk of raw meat. Blood was dripping from her fingers onto the ground. Ebony took a closer look and realised that it was not just meat, but a heart, which the queen grasped firmly with her claw-like hands.

Then the queen started to speak and Ebony noticed that the blood was also covering her mouth and chin.

"I'm the fairest of them all, just like it has been before. I brought about Snow White's downfall and ripped her heart out of her core. Now she'll never be fair again, because this is where her story ends."

"Nooooo!"

With a loud scream Ebony awoke from her dream. Her heart was racing, just like it had done within her nightmare. She was panting and sweating, feeling hot and cold at the same time.

She sat up straight in her bed and stared into the darkness, until she heard the hurried footsteps of her chambermaid approaching the door.

"Lady Ebony?" The chambermaid knocked on the door. "Is everything all right, my lady?"

"Yes, I'm fine," Ebony replied, trying to sound calm. "Just a nightmare. Sorry to have woken you."

"Shall I come in?"

"No, thank you. I'm fine, really."

"If you say so."

The chambermaid sounded worried, but didn't enter the room.

Ebony waited until she heard the footsteps retreat. Then she climbed out of bed and walked towards the window, letting her gaze travel up to the distant stars. *Oh mother. Why did you have to leave us so early? Nothing of this would have happened if you had been with us. Snow White would still be here and maybe you could have even convinced father to let me leave and live a quiet life with Viola. But without you, everything has turned into a nightmare.*

Her vision blurred and she saw the images from her dream flash before her mind's eye. Then the vision changed and suddenly she saw a different image of the queen, standing within her secret chamber and talking to her magic mirror. *Am I still dreaming?*

Colours and sound flashed through her mind, until she was sure that this was not a dream. *Those are memories! The ones I had forgotten – about the queen – and how she ordered the huntsman to kill Snow White.*

Another memory appeared within her mind, of Henry the huntsman, who told her how he had spared Snow White's life and left her in the woods. *Henry! Of course! He led me into the forest and told me about the queen's order. But the queen found out that Snow White is alive. She's probably planning to kill her right now!*

All sleepiness drained from Ebony's body and left her wide awake, her heart pounding and the blood rushing through her ears. *I've got to stop her before she succeeds. I couldn't take it to lose Snow White for good! Not her, too. I've got to put an end to this. But how?*

Thoughts and fragments of memories flashed through her mind, but no useful idea as how to stop the queen was to be found anywhere inside her head.

There was no time to lose though and thus Ebony decided to check on the queen first, while she tried to come up with a workable plan.

As quietly as possible she left her chamber and tiptoed through the castle until she reached the south tower. The door to the sleeping chamber of the queen was closed and no sound could be heard from the inside. *If she is as perfect as she makes everyone believe, I'm sure she wouldn't snore. I've got to take a look inside to see whether she's up to something.*

Ebony held her breath while she pushed down the doorhandle as gently as her fingers were capable of. Luckily the door didn't make a sound as it swung open. Ebony peeked through the crack in the door and tried to make out the sleeping silhouette of the queen. Her bed seemed to be empty though. Ebony furrowed her brow. *Could she be within her secret chamber right now, planning how to kill my sister?*

She hesitated for a few seconds, but her head hadn't come up with any kind of useful plan so far and left her no choice but to venture forward.

Her heart picked up its speed, while her feet took every step very slowly and carefully, trying not to make a sound. That way, holding her breath whenever she thought to hear something, Ebony made her way into the queen's chamber.

Even on closer examination, the queen was nowhere to be seen. With growing anticipation, Ebony sneaked up the stone staircase and looked into every single chamber on her way. They were all empty and dark, even the secret chamber at the top, as far as she could make out through the keyhole.

For a split second, Ebony thought about trying to unlock the door and stepping in front of the magic mirror to ask it where Snow White and the queen might be, but she quickly gave up on that again. *Who knows how the mirror will react? It might turn me into a toad with its dark magic! Or alarm the queen and tell her what I know. That would probably be the end of me. Not to mention that I have no clue how to open that door.*

Not wishing to die by the hands of the queen, Ebony retreated back into her own chamber. It was still dark outside and her eyes reminded her that she had barely slept so far. Her heart and mind didn't really want to rest though while Snow White was in danger.

With a sigh, Ebony lay down on her bed and closed her eyes, trying to recall everything she knew about the queen and Snow White's disappearance. She was relieved that her memories now returned effortlessly to her and her mind didn't get clouded and distracted anymore once she started to think about this topic. *Maybe the queen has been influencing me with her dark magic. Can she read my mind? Or mess with my thoughts? But where is she now?!*

More and more questions bubbled up in her head, while the answers hid behind the cover of uncertainty. At some point, Ebony fell asleep again, tossing and turning restlessly in her bed, while dark nightmares haunted her sleep.

$\mathfrak{At}$ the crack of dawn, Ebony woke up with a start, the image of Snow White's dead body still fresh before her mind's eye. *It was just a dream. Only a nightmare – not reality.*

She breathed fitfully and it took a couple of minutes until she had convinced herself that Snow White still had to be alive. *Viola said that twins have a special connection between them. And even if I might not have felt it before, I'm sure I would know it if Snow White was murdered.*

While the memories of the last night returned and replaced the gruesome images of her nightmare, her head reminded her that Snow White still might be in immediate danger right now. *I've got to find her before the queen can get to her. I've got to go back into the forest.*

As soon as she had made up her mind, Ebony scrambled out of bed and dressed herself as quickly as possible. The day was still young and the king fast asleep within his chamber. Ebony could hear his snoring in the hallway as she passed his door. *If he would only believe me! But he never will. He'd probably think I'm crazy if I told him about the magic mirror. I have to do this on my own.*

She stopped in front of the queen's chamber and put a trembling hand upon the doorhandle. Her heart was just as nervous as her fingers and drowned out the sound of her breathing. *I just hope that no one will see me.*

Just as the night before the door swung open silently and enabled Ebony to peek inside the circular room. It was empty. *Where could she have gone? Is she already inside the woods? Does she know where Snow White is hiding?*

Panic arose inside her. *What am I supposed to do now? I can't just ride into the forest on a wing and a prayer. I didn't find her last time, even though Henry pointed out the direction to me. If I go back there all on my own, I'll probably get lost for good and die of exhaustion while the queen gets to Snow White and – No! I can't let that happen.*

With a lump in her throat, Ebony stepped inside the queen's chamber and crept up the south tower until she reached the top. The wooden door was closed, but not locked. *Huh. That's strange. Wasn't it locked last night?* As Ebony thought about it, she noticed that she hadn't even tried to open the door the night before. *In the beginning, the queen always locked it when she wasn't inside. Is she getting sloppy? Or could this be a trap?*

There was no way of finding out without trying. Ebony gathered all her courage and stepped inside the secret chamber. Nothing happened. *So far, so good.*

Her heart started to race as she stepped in front of the magic mirror and looked at her worried reflection. It looked as pale as ever, but with dark circles under her eyes. *Well, at least I'm not a toad yet. Here goes nothing …*

"Mirror, mirror, on the wall – um – who's the fairest of them all?"

Ebony held her breath and prayed that the mirror would either ignore her or spare her life at least. *I don't want to end up as an enchanted animal.*

At first it looked like nothing was going to happen at all, but then her reflection suddenly started to change. The dark circles vanished and her cheeks started to look rosy, while her hair seemed to grow at an incredible speed, until it framed her curved body with long, red curls. *What's happening? Am I being enchanted after all??*

Ebony looked down on herself, but she couldn't make out any changes. Her hair was barely reaching her bosom, which was still rather flat. *Is this an illusion? Does the mirror want to scare me away?*

Then the beautiful version of herself opened her perfectly curved red lips and spoke with the dark voice of the mirror that Ebony had heard before, when eavesdropping on the queen.

"Snow White is the fairest to be seen, but soon she'll be dead by the hands of the queen."

"What? No! That can't – how? Where is she? Snow White I mean? Can you tell me?"

"She's deep in the forest, hard to be found, for there are no tracks or clues on the ground. But if you listen to the birds and follow their song, you will soon find the one for whom you so long."

"The birds? I have to follow the birds? But there are hundreds of them in the forest! How will I know which ones to follow?"

"The happiest tune, with the scent of flowers, purer than anything within these towers, will show you the way, if you're true at heart, because nothing keeps loving siblings apart."

Ebony stared blankly at the mirror. Her thoughts were racing, while doubt and fear added to the chaos in her head. *Follow the birds? I might as well search the whole forest with a hundred men and probably be luckier.*

"Couldn't you just tell me where she is?" Ebony pleaded with desperation in her voice. "Is she with someone? Or lost in the woods? Is there something specific I can look for? A house, a hut, a stream –"

"Seven dwarves are her hosts right now, no danger within their home they allow. But while they're gone, evil will strike. So you'd better get going and start the hike."

"Dwarves?!"

The magic mirror stayed silent and Ebony was sure that he wasn't willing to give out any more information.

"Thank you," she mumbled while she turned around and dashed down the stone steps. This time she didn't care to be silent. If the magic mirror had spoken the truth, the queen wasn't within her chambers anyway, but rather on her way to killing Snow White. *I've got to hurry! If she gets to Snow White before me, I'll lose another person who is precious to me. I can't let that happen!*

Ebony didn't meet anyone as she left the queen's chamber, but on her way to her own room, she bumped into her father, who was going the other way.

"Hold your horses! What's the rush, my dear? Aren't you coming to breakfast?"

His eyes scrutinised her face and seemed to pick up some of the panic which Ebony instantly tried to hide. His brows furrowed and a look of worry appeared on his face.

"Ebony, my dear, is something the matter? You look like you've seen a ghost –"

"Well, something like that. It's just – have you seen the queen lately? Since yesterday evening, I mean?"

"No, not really. She said she was tired and retreated into her chambers rather early. She also said that she didn't feel all too well and might not attend breakfast this morning. Why?"

"Huh. Just wondering." *Very convenient to act like she's sick. I wonder how long it will take for him to notice that she has vanished from the castle?*

"Are you sure that there is nothing else?" the king asked and eyed her closely. "You don't look too healthy yourself. You're rather pale –"

"I haven't slept much. A few nightmares kept me awake and – well – I was –" *How can I say this without arousing suspicion??*

"You can talk to me about anything, my dear," the king assured her with an encouraging but worried smile. "You know that, right?"

"Sure. Thank you, father. It's just – I was up early because of the nightmares and – when I passed the queen's chamber –"

"You went to the south tower?"

"Yes. And I think that she's gone."

"What?"

"I – well – I thought that I heard something suspicious from within –" *Namely absolutely nothing.* "– and I took a look inside –"

"You spied on the queen?" the king exclaimed with shock in his eyes.

"No. I just wanted to make sure that she's all right. But she wasn't inside her chamber and I haven't met her yet."

Ebony looked at her father with pleading eyes. *If I can get him to search for the queen, we might as well catch her on her way to Snow White and prevent the worst from happening. But we have to hurry!*

"She's not within her chamber?" the king repeated surprised and furrowed his brows even further. "That's strange. But maybe she's just feeling better and has already gone to the breakfast table. We should check there first before we jump to conclusions."

Worry clouded his face as he started to walk at a brisk pace towards the dining room. Ebony followed him and hoped that the king would soon announce a search of the whole area around the castle, including the forest nearby.

When they reached the dining room and found it empty though, the king did not run towards the south tower to check on the queen – as Ebony had hoped – but sat down instead and indicated to her to do the same.

"But father –"

"I'll send someone to check on the queen. But I don't want to imagine or worry about any of my loved ones being lost before breakfast. It's not good to worry on an empty stomach."

With that, the king started to eat and Ebony forced herself to do the same. *If I just run away now, he's going to stop me for sure. And I will need all of my strength to get to Snow White in time, so I might as well eat while I still have the chance.*

Ebony ate as quickly as possible and even managed to let some pieces of bread slip into her sleeves, which she was planning to take with her into the forest. When breakfast was over, the king's servant returned and informed him that the queen was indeed not inside her chambers.

"For the love of God!" the king exclaimed with worry in his voice. "Why do people have to go missing right within this castle all the time?"

Just as Ebony had hoped, the king instantly ordered a search of the whole castle area.

Ebony didn't want to wait for them to find out that the queen was gone though. Time was short and she used the following commotion to sneak into the kitchen to get some more food and some water for her journey.

Then she slipped out into the garden and waited until everyone was inside to search the castle. Even the guards on the walls were busy with the search and not paying enough attention to notice Ebony, as she slipped behind the curtain of vine tendrils.

With some difficulty, she opened the hidden wooden door just wide enough for her to slip through and pulled it shut again as soon as she had stepped into the stone paved tunnel. Impenetrable darkness surrounded her and robbed her of any sense of direction.

She stumbled forward until she felt the cold walls of the tunnel to her left. With one hand upon the wall, she walked on as fast as she could and hoped that she would reach the forest in time. *Hang in there, Snow White. I'm coming!*

𝕯𝖊𝖊𝖕 in the forest, further than any men went, Snow White was airing the beds of the dwarves, who had already gone to work in the mines. Just as she took out the blankets to shake them out, she heard someone approach from the thicket.

She left the blankets outside and quickly withdrew into the house, shutting the door behind her and peeking outside one of the tiny windows. It took only a few seconds until a hunched figure stepped out of the woods, cloaked in a battered coat, the hood hiding the face within dark shadows.

Snow White watched as the hunched figure slowly wobbled towards the little hut and knocked on the door.

"Who is it?" Snow White called out and held her breath.

"Just an elderly farmer's widow who seeks a glass of water and a chair to rest upon," a croaky voice replied. "My old bones are tired from the journey and I have run out of water."

"There are wooden chairs outside on which you can rest, good woman," replied Snow White and watched the hooded person through the window. "I'm not allowed to step outside and keep you company, but there is a well in the garden from which you can drink as much as you want."

"Thank you, my dear," the hunched figure answered. "But could you give me a mug or cup to drink from? I'm afraid I don't have anything with me –"

"Of course. I will pass it to you through the window."

Snow White hurried to the kitchen cupboard and picked up a mug, which she then handed to the elderly woman, which waited in front of the window.

"That's very kind of you, my dear," the croaky voice thanked her from under the hood. "Are you sure you don't want to step outside? It's a lovely day and the sun is smiling upon us. You see, I haven't had much company since my husband died and now I'm all alone with no one to talk to. It gets very lonely, I can tell you."

"I'm sorry, but I can't."

"Well, if you insist," the old woman sighed heavily. "But you've been so very kind to me. Let me at least repay you for your hospitality. Here, see? I have some tasty fresh apples from my own garden. Would you like to try one?"

"No, thank you, I –"

"Please!" crooned the old lady. "I insist."

"All right. But just one. Thank you."

Snow White accepted the red apple that the hooded woman gave to her. It looked ripe and delicious, but Snow White couldn't help thinking of the dwarves warning not to trust anyone.

"Don't you want to take a bite?" the old woman asked susurrant. "I can assure you, they are fresh and *very* good."

"I don't know –"

"Not the trusting type, are you? Well, let's make a deal: I'll eat one half of the apple and you'll take the other one. That way we both share a delicious meal, all right?"

Snow White nodded hesitantly and let the old woman cut the apple in half. She noticed that one part of the apple was not as red and perfect as the other, but didn't bother to worry about it.

"There we go," the croaky voice stated. "You take the sweet red half. It fits to your beautiful lips."

Snow White took the half which was offered to her and couldn't help but feel a deep urge to take a bite. The red colour of the apple looked mouth-watering, but she restrained herself and waited until the old woman had taken a bite of her own paler half.

Satisfied and assured that the apple had to be harmless, Snow White then took a bite of her own half. It did indeed taste very sweet – too sweet. The taste clouded her mind and made her feel dizzy. She hastily tried to swallow the piece to get rid of the sweetness in her mouth, but it got stuck in her throat and made her choke.

Her eyes bulging, Snow White turned towards the window and looked at the old woman for help. But there was no hooded figure anymore.

Instead, the malicious grin of the queen shone down upon her as Snow White fell to the ground. Her vision blurred and the last thing she heard was the triumphant laugh of the queen, which seemed to pierce Snow White's heart. Then her mind was clouded in darkness and her consciousness faded away, until there was everlasting blackness and silence.

Ebony stumbled and fell onto the forest floor. Her feet were tired, as was the rest of her exhausted body, but she forced herself to get up again and kept running. She hadn't stopped ever since she had left the darkness of the tunnel behind.

Trees and bushes were surrounding her from all sides and looked alike wherever she went, but she kept going, determined to reach Snow White before it was too late.

Her ears had picked up the sound of the singing birds as soon as she had made her first steps into the woods and she had been following them ever since. At first it had been hard to make out the most cheerful song over the sound of her running feet, but she had gotten used to it by now and followed the voices of the birds as fast as she could.

But not only the songs of the birds gave her clues. Some ravens and crows came to her aid from time to time, flying in front of her for a little while to guide her in the right direction.

Around midday, she had to take a small break to recover a little and gather new strength, but even then she kept walking at a brisk pace while she ate and drank some of her supplies.

She was just about to start running again, when she suddenly heard the sound of snapping twigs. *Could that be the queen? Have I caught up with her? Or is she already on her way back?*

Ebony didn't dare to think the latter through to the end. She hid behind the trunk of a tree and kept an eye on the thicket from which the sound had come. It didn't take long until she heard it again. *Sounds like footsteps. But too heavy for the queen. Rather like several feet. Could father's search troops have come after me?*

It took only a few seconds until she got an answer.

Two heartbeats later, a gigantic male boar stepped out of the thicket. His huge canine teeth made him look rather impressive and Ebony couldn't help but admire his massive appearance.

The boar seemed to sense his admirer and looked into her direction with dark brown eyes which appeared to be as deep as the forest itself.

Both of them stood very still for a while, until the boar took a few steps into her direction and met her gaze with calm serenity.

Encouraged by his lack of fear, Ebony stepped forward from behind the trunk of the tree and slowly walked towards the boar, until they were only a few paces apart. Then she stopped and waited for his reaction.

He just eyed her for a couple of seconds – and then something very unexpected happened.

The boar lowered his front legs and turned his head so that his canine teeth gave away the path to his back.

"Do you want me to climb onto your back?" Ebony whispered with disbelief in her voice. "Am I supposed to ride with you? Can you take me to Snow White?"

Of course, the boar didn't answer any of those questions. He just waited and looked at her with encouraging eyes. *Well, I'll take that as a yes.*

Ebony stepped forward, her heart beating fast with curious excitement, and climbed very carefully onto the furry back of the huge animal. *I love horse riding, but this is even more fun!*

As soon as she had positioned herself upon his back, the boar got up and turned around, carrying her deep into the forest. He quickly picked up speed and soon they were dashing through the thickets like deer fleeing from a hunting party. Ebony could still faintly hear the song of the birds and sometimes saw a raven above them and thus was sure that the boar was taking her into the right direction.

They rode on like this for quite a while and Ebony nearly lost track of time. Only the sun, which was now moving towards the horizon again, told her that it had to be late in the afternoon already. The boar didn't seem to get tired though and kept running, until he finally slowed down and walked the last bit at a normal pace.

When they stepped onto a clearing, Ebony instantly knew that it had to be the dwarves' home of which the mirror had been talking. A small hut stood in the middle of the meadow, surrounded by vegetable patches, flowerbeds and a wooden fence, which was covered with eight blankets. *Looks like someone is at home and airing the beds. Could it be my sister?*

As the boar halted, Ebony didn't even wait for it to lower it's back again, but just jumped down and dashed towards the small hut. Then she stopped, turned around, bowed to the boar with a breathless "Thank you" and spun around to get to the entrance of the wooden hut.

"Hello? Is anyone home?"

She knocked on the door several times, her heart racing and her head spinning. *Please open the door. Please!*

Behind her, the boar slowly retreated into the woods, leaving Ebony alone with her worries and fears. She waited for a couple of seconds, then she knocked again.

"Snow White? Are you in there? It's me, Ebony!"

No answer.

"Please open the door!"

Silence.

147

Ebony knocked a third time, this time hammering against the small door with both fists and calling out for her sister at the top of her voice.

"Snow White! Let me in! Please! I beg of you. It's me, Ebony, your little sister. Open the door!"

Her calls stayed unanswered and desperation started to overwhelm the young princess. Silent tears rolled down her pale cheeks and dropped onto the ground. As she followed them with her gaze, she noticed several pairs of footprints just beside the house.

There were traces of many small feet, which had to belong to the dwarves. But there were two pairs of normal sized footprints: one of small, elegant, light feet and another of heavier shoes. *Someone with boots or clunky footwear was here not long ago. Could it have been the huntsman? Did he decide to finish his job after all? No, the footprints are too small for a man of his size. Could it have been the queen then? Maybe in disguise?*

A sense of foreboding crept down Ebony's spine and let her heart miss a beat. An icy chill flowed through her veins and made her shiver, even though the rays of the low sun were still warming the air.

With trembling fingers, Ebony pushed down the handle of the entrance door and opened it, holding her breath as she looked inside. It was rather dark and her eyes couldn't make out much at first. She took a few steps forward, but then she froze to the spot, staring down onto the ground with wide eyes.

No.

Her heart missed another beat.

No!

Her head started to spin, while her lungs forgot how to work properly.

"NO!"

Her loud scream echoed through the hut and the forest. The birds stopped singing for a moment of shock, while Ebony fell down onto her knees beside the lifeless body of her beloved sister.

"No – this can't be – Please! Don't be dead. I need you! Please – come back to me –"

She started to sob uncontrollably, her body shaking violently, while a veil of salty tears clouded her view. Her hands trembled as bad as never before as she reached for her sister's pale cheek.

"Please, Snow White. Wake up!"

She caressed the beautiful face with gentle fingers, searching for a sign of life. The rosy colour had vanished from her sister's face though and no breath moved the well-curved bosom.

"Please, don't leave me."

Ebony kissed the forehead of her motionless sister, tears dripping down on the cold face. Snow White's eyes were closed, as if she was just sleeping, but Ebony could feel that this was not the case.

Still trembling, she laid one hand onto her sister's chest. There was no heartbeat, no movement, no sign of life. Snow White was dead.

𝔚𝔥𝔦𝔩𝔢 Ebony was mourning the death of her sister, the queen was hurrying back to the castle, eager to finally get the answer from the magic mirror for which her jealous heart was longing.

The feeling of victory and triumph seemed to lend wings to her feet and let her reach the castle shortly after nightfall. She used the secret tunnel to get into the castle grounds unnoticed, but to her surprise the exit into the flower garden was manned with two guards.

She quickly recoiled into the shadows before they noticed her and got rid of her disguise, which she left in the dark tunnel. Then she stepped out with as much dignity as only a queen can muster and met the surprised gaze of the two guards.

"Your majesty," one of them stammered, "where have you been? The king has been searching for you all day long. And lady Ebony is gone as well."

"My affairs are none of your business," the queen replied icily. "I shall only speak to my husband about where I have been. Let me through!"

Her commanding voice made the two men jump. They stepped aside very quickly and let the queen enter the castle without further ado.

Instead of going to the king, the queen slipped into the south tower though and hastened up the stone staircase to her secret chamber. It was unlocked and she chided herself for being so careless, but didn't bother to worry about it. She trusted that neither the king nor the servants would be bold enough to come up here.

With long strides she stepped in front of her magic mirror and smiled at her own flawless reflection.

"Mirror, mirror, on the wall, who is the fairest of us all?"

"The fairest one is you my queen, now that Snow White has fallen prey to your scheme."

"Yes, she did indeed!" triumphed the queen joyfully. "Now no one will ever rival my beauty again. And if it's true that this wretched little redhead is gone, too, I'll have the king all to myself."

The queen's evil laughter rang through the south tower and in the ears of the young fairy apprentice, who was watching the events through one of the mirrors within the Chamber of Sight.

The Good Fairy had returned from her journey as well and together they had witnessed the murder of Snow White and Ebony's desperate try to save her sister.

Now that the queen seemed to have won, the young fairy couldn't help but cry a few silent tears, because she could not bear to see Ebony in despair.

"You said that it would all end well," she sobbed and looked at the Good Fairy with accusing eyes. "You said that the queen would be punished eventually. But now Snow White is dead, Ebony is heartbroken and the queen has all the chances in the world to poison the king's heart with her evil words."

"I never said that *all* would end well," argued the Good Fairy with a calm voice. "I merely said that life can set everything right over time."

"But how should any of this ever be turned right again? Snow White is dead!"

"Is she now?"

The young fairy looked at her mistress with confusion.

"Um – yes. She is – Isn't she?"

"Look closer," the Good Fairy ordered and pointed at the mirror, which showed Ebony weeping over her dead

151

sister. "Look with your magic and you'll see what the human eye can't detect."

Arabella tried to follow the order of the Good Fairy and stared at said mirror with furrowed brows and utmost concentration.

"Wait!" she then exclaimed. "I can feel her heartbeat. It's nearly not detectable, but it's there. Her heart is still beating. And she's even breathing! But how can that be?"

"The queen gave Snow White the poisoned half of the apple," the Good Fairy started to explain. "But the poison she chose can only take full effect if it enters the digestive system. Snow White didn't swallow any part of her half of the apple though. It got stuck in her throat – and that's where it still is."

"But doesn't that mean that she choked on it? Isn't she going to suffocate if that thing is stuck there?"

"No. There is still enough air getting into her body to survive for a while," the Good Fairy corrected her excited apprentice. "Some of the poison must have entered her stomach with the saliva and made her fall into something like a coma. Her heart rate has dropped a lot, so it won't kill her that she doesn't breathe properly."

"And how long can she survive like this?"

"Who knows?" the Good Fairy asked and sat down in her armchair to watch the mirrors in a more comfortable position. "We'll have to be patient and find out."

The dwarves were heartbroken when they came home and found Snow White dead on the floor. At first, they thought that Ebony had killed her and accused her to be a witch, but then they noticed the tears and pain on the young woman's face.

"It must have been the evil queen," they mused and sat down beside Ebony. "We warned Snow White that she should be careful. But that witch must have found a way to trick her."

"The door was closed when I came here," Ebony explained with a lump in her throat. "But the window was open. Maybe the queen gave her a poison to drink or bewitched her with an evil spell."

She couldn't make herself picture the scene clearly in her head. It would have involved admitting that her sister was gone for good and she was not yet ready for that challenge.

"Even in death, she is still beautiful," one of the dwarves whispered.

"She looks like she's sleeping," mouthed another.

Then they sat silently around Snow White's lifeless body and wept and mourned and grieved over her. Ebony stayed with them, not able to leave her sister's side. The dwarves brought her water from time to time, but she wouldn't accept anything to eat.

Thus, they sat beside Snow White all night, enlightened by the flickering light of candles and the silvery glow of the moon. As the moonlight fell through the window and onto Snow White's face, Ebony could have sworn that her sister was merely sleeping. She looked peaceful and calm, as if no harm in the world could trouble her.

Time dragged on and Ebony's eyes got tired, but she didn't want to leave her sister and stayed where she was, until the first light of dawn started to enlighten the sky outside the window.

"Should we bury her within the woods?" one of the dwarves asked quietly, but all the others shook their heads.

"No," the youngest dwarf said. "She's too beautiful to hide her in the ground."

"We should make a glass coffin for her," another dwarf suggested with a husky voice.

"Yes. That way we could always look at her and never forget her lovely face."

Ebony stayed silent while the dwarves got busy. Her heart wasn't willing to accept her sister's death yet, even though everything she heard and saw told her that it was too late for a rescue. *Too late. I was too late. I couldn't save you, my beloved sis. And now it's too late for anything.*

Fresh tears rolled down her cheeks, while she caressed the soft cheeks and the long ebony hair. *The dwarves are right. You look like you're sleeping. Not even death could rob you of your beauty. Will you stay like this forever?*

Ebony kept losing herself in thoughts of grief and longing, while the dwarves distracted themselves by making a glass coffin for the deceased princess.

When it was ready early next day, Snow White still hadn't lost any of her beauty except being rather pale and Ebony hadn't left her side for more than a few minutes. She kissed her sister on the cheek again, before allowing the dwarves to put her into the glass coffin and decorating her deathbed with flowers.

Snow White then looked even more like she was only sleeping, embedded in a bed of roses, her favourites while she had been alive.

"Where will you put the coffin?" Ebony forced herself to ask, while she still couldn't take her eyes off her sister.

"We will carry it to a nearby meadow. It's all covered with flowers and always crowded with butterflies. Snow White loved to go there when we were around to keep watch over her."

Ebony nodded and followed the dwarves to said meadow, which was even more beautiful than she had imagined it. *Snow White must have loved it here. She could have been happy, if the queen had not pursued her. If she only hadn't been so damn beautiful to arouse such envy.*

Neither Ebony nor the dwarves could make themselves leave when they had put down the coffin onto a bed of soft grass. They all stood around the sparkling glass, admiring Snow White's beauty, which barely had started to falter.

Only in the evening, the dwarves managed to persuade Ebony to leave her sister's side and follow them back to their home, where they made her eat a bit of soup and drink some warm tea.

It didn't help to make her feel better and not even the hot tea was able to chase away the icy cold, which had settled down inside her chest. She thanked the dwarves anyway and accepted their offer to sleep in the bed they had made for Snow White.

One of the dwarves went out after dinner and guarded the glass coffin, making sure that no more harm would come to their beloved princess.

From that day on, the dwarves guarded the glass coffin every day and night, taking turns and being accompanied by Ebony during daytime.

"Don't you want to return to your father?" the dwarves asked after a few days, but Ebony shook her head.

"I can't go back to the castle," Ebony sobbed. "I couldn't face the queen without telling everyone what she did. But I don't have any proof. Nobody would believe me."

"Not even your father?"

"Especially him. He loves the queen and is bewitched by her beauty. He would probably think that I've gone mad over the loss of my sister."

"Well, you are welcome to stay with us as long as you want," offered the dwarves and Ebony gladly accepted their invitation.

She helped them in the household sometimes, but most of the time, she sat beside her sister's glass coffin or lay in the grass beside it, watching the butterflies, birds and clouds pass by.

Time seemed to stay still within the coffin and Snow White's face didn't wither or lose any of its beauty. Only the pale cheeks told Ebony that her sister wasn't asleep, but she still found herself hoping that some miracle would occur and wake Snow White from her eternal slumber.

𝔐𝔞𝔫𝔶 days and nights passed, while Ebony lost track of time and lust for life. She barely remembered the happy days within the castle gardens, where she had played with her sister and laughed amongst the flowers.

Now all the colour seemed to drain from the world and neither the flowers nor the animals of the forest could cheer her up. The red of her sister's lips was the only colour she still saw and that of the roses, which the dwarves always renewed before the old ones could even wither.

Summer passed and was about to turn into autumn, as one day, a prince and his men passed by the meadow on their way through the forest. They had lost their path and just stopped to ask for the way, but as the young prince laid eyes on Snow White, he was instantly struck by her undying beauty.

"Who is this?" he asked as he dismounted his horse and stepped closer to the glass coffin.

"It's my sister, Snow White," answered Ebony with pain in her voice. "She was killed by a witch and left to lie in an eternal slumber, never aging or fading."

The prince was charmed by what he saw, but shocked by what he heard.

"Killed by a witch? How gruesome! To rob such beauty of the spark of life – an unforgivable crime."

Ebony nodded and eyed the prince, before she turned back to her sister. *You would have liked him, sis. He's handsome and charming. Maybe he would have even been your love at first sight.*

While she was lost in thoughts, the prince greeted the oldest dwarf and asked for a way out of the woods. When it was time to part again, the young lad couldn't bring himself to part from Snow White and her stunning beauty though.

"Please, fair lady and kind dwarf, allow me to take Snow White with me to my father's kingdom. I'll take good care of her, I promise."

At first, neither the dwarf nor Ebony could agree to part with Snow White. The dwarf said he would miss the fair sight of the princess too much and Ebony made the point that it would be rather weird to give the body of her beloved sister to a stranger.

But the prince begged them to have mercy with his heart, which was deeply in love with Snow White. Thus, the other six dwarves were summoned and together they argued for quite a while.

In the end, the dwarves were willing to let go of Snow White, because they sensed true love within the prince's words. Only Ebony didn't want to part from her sister.

"I couldn't just let her go," she whispered. "She's all I have left. Please don't take her away from me."

The prince was moved by her words and the agony in her voice, even though he couldn't make himself look into her black eyes for long.

"If you don't want to part from your sister, you might as well accompany me to my father's kingdom. I'm sure you would be welcome to stay there as our guest in exchange for the honour of having your beautiful sister with us."

Ebony shot a glance at the dwarves, who nodded encouragingly.

"All right. I'll accept your offer and come with you."

The prince thanked her and the dwarves for their kindness and ordered his men to pick up the glass coffin. They carefully carried it upon their shoulders and set off into the woods again.

Ebony accompanied them and one of the prince's men even offered her his horse so that she wouldn't have to walk all the way.

The dwarves followed them as well, not yet ready to part from Snow White. They wanted to make sure that she would be safe and cared for and thus walked alongside the glass coffin for a short while.

Just when they had finally said their goodbyes and were about to go back to their hut, one of the king's men stumbled over a tree root and fell to the forest floor.

The glass coffin came tumbling down behind him, but the other men were able to catch it and keep it from shattering on the ground.

Ebony held her breath and looked for a crack in the glass, but there was none. The roses had been messed up by the concussion though – and not just them.

The jolt had also loosened the piece of apple which had been stuck in Snow White's throat. Ebony noticed it, because the perfect red edge of the apple piece showed between Snow White's flawlessly white teeth.

"Put down the coffin," Ebony demanded and jumped from her horse to run to her sister. "I think she can still be saved! She might yet be alive!"

And she was indeed.

While the surrounding men watched her curiously, Ebony was busy opening the glass coffin and pulled the piece of poisoned apple out of Snow White's mouth.

"That's what the witch must have used to poison her," she exclaimed and held the piece of apple high for everyone to see. "It got stuck in her throat and made her appear dead."

Under the astonished eyes of the prince and the dwarves, Ebony bent over her sister's body and listened for a sign of life. She watched Snow White closely and soon noticed that the rosy colour started to return to her soft cheeks again.

"She's alive!" Ebony cheered and softly caressed the face of her sister, which was finally feeling warm again. "You came back to me."

As if reacting to her little sister's gentle touch, Snow White started to breathe deeply again. Then she suddenly opened her eyes and coughed, trying to sit up.

"Some water. Quick!"

Ebony signalled one of the prince's men to give her his water hose and helped her sister to moisten her dry throat. Snow White drank a few sips, but then her eyes fell upon the prince. She stopped drinking, her eyes widening.

"Ebby?" she whispered. "Am I in Heaven?"

"No, just plain old Earth." Ebony grinned. "Or maybe your personal heaven on earth. I thought that you might like him. Is that what love on first sight feels like?"

Snow White nodded, her gaze locked with that of the prince, who had gotten down from his horse and approached the two princesses with a polite smile.

"I don't mean to interrupt, but –"

"Well, you are interrupting," Ebony stated sternly. "Could you please give us a minute? There are a few things I'd like to ask my sister, before you two can properly fall in love, all right?"

"Um – of course."

The prince blushed, but stepped back and waited, while Ebony turned back to Snow White, who couldn't take her eyes off the prince though.

That changed quickly as Ebony suddenly hugged her sister very tightly and pressed her cheek against the warm skin, which smelled of roses and life.

"I'm so glad that you're back, big sis! I thought I had lost you too. Did the queen do this to you?"

"She did indeed."

All the memories came flashing back to Snow White and she gasped as she remembered her near-death experience. A shudder ran down her spine, but she forced herself to tell Ebony how the queen had tricked her.

"She made you eat half an apple?" Ebony furrowed her brows. "I bet it was poisoned. At least your half. That way she could eat the harmless half herself and convince you to take a bite. But why didn't you die?"

"Shouldn't you just be happy about it?"

"I am! But I still don't understand. What exactly happened when you swallowed your half of the apple?"

"I never really got a chance to do so," Snow White admitted. "It was so awfully sweet that it clouded my mind. I choked on it, because it got stuck in my throat."

"Huh. That would explain it – maybe. Your body stayed the same, because you were still alive – only in a deep sleep due to the bit of poison that you probably swallowed."

Snow White stared at her little sister with wide eyes.

"You mean – If I had swallowed all of it – I would be dead now?"

"I believe so," answered Ebony with a grim face. "And I'm sure the queen won't like that you've woken up. She'll most likely come after you again –"

"No," the prince stepped in. "I won't let that happen!"

He approached Snow White with the spark of love in his eyes and a look of determination on his face.

"Please, fair Snow White. Let me take you to my kingdom and protect you from any harm that might try to follow you. I swear I won't let this evil witch – Wait! You called her a queen?"

"Yes," Ebony replied quickly. "She has bewitched and married our father, the king. She would stop at nothing to get my sister killed."

"Well, in that case you should both accompany me to my father's kingdom," the prince insisted, "where I can keep you safe. She won't be allowed to follow you there if I tell my father what she has done to you, fair Snow White."

"Yes," Snow White breathed with a joyful smile. "That would be wonderful."

"What?" Ebony stared at her with disbelief. "But we can't just let our father behind! We have to warn him of the evil within his new wife. Otherwise, she'll poison the whole kingdom with her wrath, once she finds out that you are alive. We have to go back and confront her – together."

"Then I shall accompany you," the prince offered. "I won't let any harm come to Snow White ever again."

"Very kind of you," Ebony said with a snort. "But we have to be careful. Who knows what kinds of wicked magic this evil person has in store?"

"I don't fear any witch nor danger when it comes to protecting the love of my life."

The prince smiled at Snow White and she returned his smile with sparkling eyes. *Gosh! The two are sweeter than a poisoned apple. I just hope that they won't make mooneyes at each other all the way.*

"We'll come with you," the dwarves offered and hurried to Snow White's side, while the prince helped her out of the glass coffin.

"Thank you very much," Ebony replied, smiling at them fondly. "We take all the help we can get. Together we'll hopefully be able to convince the king of how evil the queen truly is."

𝕿𝖔𝖌𝖊𝖙𝖍𝖊𝖗 Ebony, Snow White, the dwarves, the prince and his men set off towards the castle. The prince, who introduced himself as George, let Snow White ride on his horse and never took his eyes off her all the way through the forest.

Ebony on the other hand decided to walk among the dwarves and tried to ignore the soulful looks the prince was giving her sister. The two of them reminded her of Viola and it pained her to think about her own feelings. *If Snow White really leaves for another kingdom, I'll have to be the heir of father's throne. And I'm not sure if he'll let me marry Viola when I'm meant to be the future queen.*

All thoughts of love and future troubles left Ebony's mind though as they finally reached the castle on the following day.

They had spent one night in the forest in the tents that the prince and his men had brought along – Snow White and Ebony had been allowed to use the prince's tent for themselves – but Ebony had barely slept. Her body was tense and worried anticipation kept her mind busy.

As they approached the castle then, her head kept imagining all kinds of ways in which the queen might try to fool the king into believing her instead of his daughters. *What if she just puts a curse onto us all? She might mess with our minds or rob us of our voice so that we can't tell the truth about her.*

When they finally reached the gates of the castle, the guards were very surprised by what they saw: both of the missing princesses, followed by a prince, soldiers and a bunch of dwarves – and all of them looking as grim as if they were walking onto a battlefield.

"Open the gates," Ebony demanded as they halted before the closed portcullis. "My sister and I have returned and bring with us noble friends, who have helped us during our time of need. And we bring important news for the king, so hasten and let us in!"

The guards instantly followed her orders and let the strange group enter the castle grounds. The prince's men stayed with the horses, while the others ventured on and found the king within the throne room.

He looked just as tired and worried as Ebony felt, but when he laid eyes on his two daughters, his face lightened up with pure joy and relief.

"Snow White! Ebony! You're back."

Forgetting all their manners and the royal etiquette, the king and his daughters ran towards each other and ended up in a tight group hug.

The prince and the dwarves waited politely, until the king finally took a step back and eyed the two princesses with a beaming smile.

"I knew you would come back. I just knew it! But Snow White – where on earth have you been? Why were you gone for so long?"

"That's what we would like to explain to you," Ebony answered for her sister. "But first we've got to know: Where is the queen right now?"

"She retreated into her chambers right after breakfast," the king replied with a look of confusion. "But I don't understand what this has got to do with her –"

"We'll explain," Ebony interrupted him. "Now follow me. Maybe the queen will do the explaining for us. Oh, and by the way: This is prince George and with him are seven noble dwarves who have helped Snow White and me quite a lot and given us shelter. Just for your information."

With that said, Ebony turned towards the door and led the way into the hallway, while the king quickly greeted prince George and the seven dwarves.

Then they all followed Ebony to the south tower, where she stopped at the door to the queen's chamber and laid a finger upon her lips.

"I ask of you to remain silent, no matter what we find in here now. Please stay quiet and don't address the queen until I give you a signal."

The king furrowed his brows again and was about to argue, but Ebony didn't even give him a chance to speak.

"Please, father. Just trust me on this. You'll see why."

Still looking confused, the king nodded and waited for Ebony to lead them onwards.

She first put an ear against the wooden door to listen whether there was anyone inside. When she heard no sound of movement, she quietly opened the door and checked the room. It was empty, just as she had expected.

Signalling the others to follow her quietly, Ebony went into the queen's chamber and led the small group up the spiral staircase, until they reached the top.

The door to the secret chamber stood ajar and they could see the queen standing in front of her magic mirror, smiling at her own reflection.

Ebony put a finger upon her lips again and then stood aside so that the others were able to watch the queen as well. They squeezed up and peaked into the chamber together, while the queen now addressed her mirror.

"Mirror, mirror, on the wall, who is the fairest of us all?"

"You are fair, my queen, that's true. But Snow White is a thousand times fairer than you."

"What? You've got to be kidding me! I have killed Snow White! She's gone for good, I know it. I've watched her die.

You've got to be mistaken! Or do dead people suddenly count as well?!"

"Snow White is alive and well. Love has overcome your spell. She lives to be the fairest of them all. Jealousy will be your own downfall."

"NO!" the queen shrieked.

Fury blazed in her eyes and with the force of fiery rage, she threw her crown against the magic mirror. The latter shattered into a million pieces, some of which hit the queen's skin and caused a dozen tiny cuts.

Ebony turned towards the others and signalled them that this was the time for action. Her father didn't have to wait for another invitation and instantly stepped into the chamber, his face a mask of cold anger.

"That's enough," he said with a booming voice and eyed the queen with disbelief. "I have loved you, made you my wife and let you into my home. And how do you repay me? Did you really try to kill Snow White?"

The queen stared at him with wide eyes, which were filled with madness and confusion.

"Darling – how did you –?"

"Don't you call me 'darling'! You tried to murder one of my beloved daughters, didn't you?"

The queen took a few steps back, until she reached the stone wall and couldn't retreat any further. She pressed her body against it as if she was hoping to disappear into the stone, while she met the angry gaze of her husband with a look of despair.

"No – I didn't – Why would you believe that?"

"Because I just heard you say it yourself when you spoke to that wicked mirror. You said that you 'killed Snow White'. And you also acted as if you did so only because my daughter was more beautiful than you. Is that true?"

"Darling – You've got to believe me – I never meant to harm you –"

"But you did! The loss of my daughters nearly killed me. Didn't you notice that? Do you only care about yourself and how you look?"

To that the queen had no answer. She stayed silent, her gaze evading that of the king, until it fell upon Ebony and the others, which were still standing in the doorway and quietly watched the scene.

"She!" the queen suddenly screamed and pointed at Ebony. "She is the evil witch! Not me. She tried to get rid of her sister, because she was jealous that you loved Snow White more than her. But she couldn't do it herself, so she threatened to bewitch me if I wouldn't help her do it. And then she nearly killed me as well. That's why I vanished into the forest for a day. It was all because of that wrecked, little, redhead witch."

She eyed Ebony with pure hatred, because she was sure that the young princess had been the one to reveal all her secrets to the king.

"Don't try to pin this on my daughter," the king warned the queen with a low voice. "You tried to do so last time, when you had wronged my people. That won't help you."

"But it's true," the queen shrieked. "Ebony is a witch. Don't you see it in her black eyes? Pure evil! As black as her heart and soul, I'm sure. And her red hair – just like blood. The blood she has on her hands for trying to murder her sister – and me!"

"Nonsense. Ebony wasn't there to threaten you minutes ago when you talked to your magic mirror and stated to have killed Snow White yourself. What is your excuse for that?"

The queen flashed her eyes at the king, but couldn't hold his gaze for long.

"I don't have to explain myself," she snapped, proudly raising her chin. "She's the evil one, not me. It's not my fault if you don't believe me."

"You *do* have to explain yourself – to me. I am the king and your husband. I command you to say the truth. Look me in the eyes and tell me: *What* is the truth?"

The king scrutinised the queen with unforgiving eyes. She tried to look at him for a few seconds, but then she turned away from him and started to cry.

"My beautiful skin – cut open – ruined – I am the one who should be pitied. Your daughters have been my downfall."

"No," the king replied calmly. "You brought all this upon yourself. Your own pride sentenced you in the end. Your heart has been spoilt by envy and jealousy – and you will have to pay the price for that."

$\mathfrak{As}$ soon as the tiny cuts on the queen's skin had received medical attention, she was brought before the king to be sentenced for her actions.

Snow White and Ebony were sitting to the left and the right of the king, while prince George and the dwarves sat beside the king's counsellors. Each of them was called forward as a witness and gave a detailed report of what they had seen and heard of the queen's misdeeds.

Once the two princesses had completed the story with their own account of the events, the queen was allowed to defend herself and asked to confess her crimes.

At first, she tried to win the king's sympathy with tears and wild stories about how she had been wronged. When that didn't work, she added some false accusations against Ebony, whom she still called a witch.

But in the end the queen noticed that no one believed her lies anymore and just admitted that she had tried to get rid of Snow White, stating that she wanted to have the king for herself.

"You didn't do it because of your jealousy then?" the king asked with an earnest voice.

"Of course not!" the queen lied. "I wouldn't send your daughter into the woods just because she's beautiful. That would be ridiculous and foolish."

"It would be indeed," the king agreed and turned towards Ebony. "But what did Henry the huntsman tell you about his mission again?"

"He said that the queen had ordered him to take Snow White deep into the forest and kill her. She also ordered him to bring back her heart, which she then would have eaten as a reward for her triumph over Snow White."

"Lies!" shrieked the queen. "You have no proof!"

Both Ebony and the king looked at the queen with stern eyes and it was obvious whom the king believed.

"I didn't lie," Ebony stated calmly. "Unlike you I don't have anything to hide. Henry the huntsman told me all this himself and if you don't admit that it's true, I'll have men search for him and bring him back here so that he can give us that proof that you demand."

The queen compressed her lips and stayed silent.

"Furthermore," Ebony continued, "the servants have confirmed that you didn't want to attend dinner on the said evening when Snow White had vanished. They told me that you had some 'private little dinner' within your room and your chambermaid confirmed that she had seen a bloody heart when she brought you a plate and cutlery."

"Well, I ate a heart then," the queen snapped. "So what? You can't proof that I actually hoped that it would be the heart of your sister."

"I saw you," Ebony interrupted the queen. "I saw you the day after. I went into your chamber, followed you up into your private room and heard you speaking to the mirror. You said that you had ordered the huntsman to kill Snow White and bring back her heart. You repeated that she was supposed to be dead several times."

The queen narrowed her eyes and hatred made her face go pale. Within her mind she was cursing herself for having been so careless and allowing Ebony to spy on her. All the hatred that once had been turned against Snow White for being fairer than the queen herself was now redirected against Ebony and the queen wished that she had killed the 'nosy princess' first so that she wouldn't have been able to cause her that much trouble.

"Do you admit to that?" the king asked sternly and eyed the queen with disappointment. "Do you admit that you hired the huntsman to kill Snow White? And that you later on tried to kill her yourself with a poisoned apple?"

The queen returned his gaze with silent fury and kept her mouth tightly shut.

"Snow White, my dear." The king turned towards his eldest daughter. "What did the huntsman tell you before you begged him to spare your life?"

"That the queen had ordered him to kill me and bring back my heart as proof that I was dead."

Snow White's voice was shaking and she couldn't help but shudder at the thought of said events.

"And what was the last thing that you saw before you lost consciousness?"

"I saw the queen. I had mistaken her for an old lady before, but she had taken her hood off by then and I could clearly see her face. She was the one who gave me the poisoned apple."

"Well," the king continued towards the queen, "it seems like everyone confirms the story which finds you guilty. You are outvoted."

He looked at the queen and waited for her answer, but she stayed silent.

"Fine. If you prefer not to answer, we'll take that as a yes, because you haven't been able to prove any of the others wrong. From this moment on, you'll be relieved of your duties as queen and will lose all rights to rule or give orders. You are not allowed to leave the castle without my permission and will be guarded day and night. You are not allowed to walk around alone, even within the castle. I'll have several of my trusted men keep a close watch on you. And your quarters will be moved from the south tower to a single chamber close to mine."

"But what about all my dresses?" the queen exclaimed in horror. "Where am I to put all my things? And what about my herbs?"

"You won't be allowed to use herbs anymore. If you require any medical attention, you are to get it from someone else. And your dresses will be stored in a chamber beside your new one. But the south tower will be opened to everyone again and will be rid of all your evil witchcraft, including the remains of your mirror."

The queen started to weep and beg, but the king wouldn't listen to her anymore. Thus, all pieces of the magic mirror were collected and destroyed for good, so that the queen would never be able to use its powers again.

$\mathfrak{Soon}$ after the queen's trial, the castle was blessed by more happy news again.

Prince George had asked the king for Snow White's hand in marriage and the king had gladly accepted, after making sure that this was his daughter's wish as well.

Snow White, of course, had been delighted and barely been able to talk about anything else since the prince had left them to travel to his home and begin the wedding preparations.

"I'm going to miss you," Ebony admitted while she walked through the gardens with her sister by her side. "Couldn't you and prince George stay here and take over father's throne?"

"No, my beloved George told me, that he is the only heir to the throne of his own father, so he has no choice but to go back – and I'll follow him wherever he goes."

"You have just returned to the castle," Ebony sighed deeply. "I can't believe that you'll soon leave it for good."

"At least the circumstances are merrier this time," Snow White argued and stopped to inhale the roses sweet scent. "But I'll miss you, too, little sis. And these gardens. I can only hope that they have flower gardens in George's kingdom as well –"

"I'm sure they do. And if not, prince George will be delighted to change that, just to make you happy. He really seems to care about you."

"Yes, he does," Snow White breathed. "And he's so handsome! I can't believe how lucky I am. He's the most adorable man I've ever seen."

Ebony rolled her eyes, but grinned.

"Combined with *your* beauty, your children will be the cutest and fairest of all."

Snow White nodded eagerly.

"I sure hope that he wants to have lots of children," she mused. "I do! Imagine sweet little George's running around. I hope they'll be as handsome as their father."

"Are looks all you ever think about?" Ebony wondered with a slight frown. "What about intelligence? Don't you want your kids to be smart? Or what about character? I sure would want my children to be honest and kind –"

"Yes, I guess that might be nice too," Snow White agreed, though it was obvious that her priorities differed from that of her sister.

"Anyway, I'll make sure to visit you often," Ebony changed the subject. "And you've got to visit me as well!"

"I will. But first we have to plan and enjoy the wedding. I can't wait to see my wedding dress. The best dress makers from all the kingdom have come together to create it. I'm so excited!"

Thus, the weeks until the wedding, which was to take place one month after the engagement, were spent in high spirits and with much enthusiasm. Not only Ebony and Snow White were glad to turn their minds towards more pleasant things in life again. All the servants rejoiced over Snow White's return to the castle and the king was as happy as any of them.

"My sweet Snow White finally getting married," he often mumbled under his breath while he walked through the castle or watched his daughters in the gardens. "My beautiful Snow White, being a bride. I just wish my beloved wife would have lived to see this day."

He often thought about his first wife now that Snow White had returned and her brown eyes reminded him of the late queen.

His new wife on the other hand was seldomly seen within the gardens and mostly stayed within her room, sulking and brooding and despising all the joy and laughter that rang through the castle.

Her gloomy presence wasn't able to cloud anyone's happiness though and when the queen announced that she wouldn't be attending the wedding, Ebony felt even more relieved. *Her jealousy wouldn't fit the occasion. And I sure don't trust her yet. She might try to poison Snow White even on her wedding day. It's better if she stays here.*

The king had his doubts about leaving the queen behind in the castle, but she insisted that she was feeling sick and wouldn't let her mind be changed about the matter.

He finally gave in, but made sure that she would be guarded by many of his best men, while he and his daughters would journey to the kingdom of prince George where the wedding was supposed to take place.

Ebony was very excited to see the foreign kingdom, while Snow White could only think about her wedding and spent most of the carriage ride raving about her beautiful white dress.

"I just hope that the weather will be nice," she mused while both she and Ebony looked out of the window, taking in the changing landscape. "It would be a shame if all the pearls and slivers of diamonds would go unnoticed due to a lack of sunlight –"

"I'm sure that the weather will be just fine," Ebony encouraged her sister. "You'll be the most glittering and sparkling sight anyone has ever seen."

And Ebony was proved right.

The wedding day of Snow White and prince George was one of the most beautiful days of autumn, with a cloudless sky, warm sunlight and a soft breeze, which rustled through the colourful leaves and made them dance to the music of the wedding celebration.

Snow White was a dazzling sight and every man who attended the wedding fell in love with her as she entered the cathedral in her sparkling white dress.

Ebony couldn't help but grin while she looked around and watched the dreamy faces of all men, who were gazing at Snow White while she walked slowly down the aisle towards her betrothed. *I bet there are a lot of men in this cathedral who wouldn't mind taking prince George's place right now.*

The lucky prince looked just as stunned as everyone else and could barely take his eyes off his bride to look at the priest for a few minutes.

When the wedding ceremony was over and the feast started, prince George had only eyes for his beautiful bride and danced with her all evening, while a lot of men stood around and watched.

Only the seven dwarves, who had been invited by Snow White herself, seemed to be as untouched by her loveliness as Ebony – even though they still admired her and cared for her deeply.

Ebony was among the standing crowd as well, mostly unnoticed in the presence of her sister, which suited her just fine. She had been keeping an eye open for Viola, but she and her parents didn't attend the wedding and she didn't dare to ask her father about it.

She just stood and watched her sister, who was smiling and radiating joy with every swirl of her dress. *Thank goodness that she didn't die! She deserves a happy ending like this. And it sure looks like she has found the love of her life – even on first sight. Some people just have it all …*

Ebony sighed and turned to walk through the vast gardens of the unfamiliar castle in which her sister would be living from now on. There were many flowers everywhere and also a large pond, to which Ebony now walked to watch the dragonflies zoom across the water.

When she had reached the edge of the pond, she looked into the deep and saw her blurred reflection staring back at her with curiosity.

Dark eyes as black as the depth of the water were surrounded by her long, red curls, which were pinned-up into an artistic hairdo. Her pale skin stood out against the darkness of the water, while her night blue dress merged perfectly with the evening sky, which was reflected by the pond's surface.

Am I like that dress? Do I merge into the crowd, unseen and unnoticed? Hard to imagine with my red hair. There's not a single redhead here, except for me. And still, I seem to be invisible to most of the guests. Snow White always stands out from the crowd – but would I want that? I don't really like being the center of attention – even though it would be nice to dance with at least ONE man who is not gaping at my sister and her beautiful dress.

With a heavy sigh, her thoughts wandered towards Viola and made her feel even more lonely. *Snow White won't come back with us. She won't be there to keep me company. And father would surely love to marry me off as soon as possible to make sure that his bloodline is secured. But would he allow me to choose Viola as my bride?*

"Why the heavy sighs?"

Ebony jumped and turned around to see who had spoken. She had been so lost in thoughts that she hadn't even noticed any approaching footsteps, but there he stood: her father, the king, a mix of joy and sorrow in his eyes.

"It's nothing," Ebony hurriedly answered. "I just – I'll miss Snow White. It feels weird to know that she'll stay here when we return to our home."

"Yes, I'll miss her too." They both sighed in unison. "But it's for the best. She'll be happy here and that's what counts. And we can visit her whenever we want."

Ebony just nodded and returned her gaze to the dragonflies. Their shiny wings shot through the warm air of the evening, while the last light of the sunset turned the sky into a sea of fiery colours. The latter were reflected by the pond and merged with Ebony's red-haired reflection, letting her hair appear to be on fire.

"Is there something else troubling your mind?"

The voice of the king was low and gentle. Ebony almost dared to give in to its comforting warmth and tell her father about her own feelings, but she couldn't bring herself to unburden her heart to him.

She turned around and tried to smile.

"No, father. I'm fine. Let's get back to the dance floor. My feet are aching for movement! Snow White is about to get some heavy dance competition."

The king returned her smile and led her back to the joyful crowd, where they danced together for a while, until finally some of the princes were able to rip their attention away from Snow White long enough to notice Ebony and ask her for a dance.

Thus, Ebony spent the rest of the evening dancing with most of the princes and even enjoyed it a little, even though she couldn't help noticing that none of them did dare to meet the gaze of her dark eyes long enough to last more than one dance.

$\mathfrak{After}$ three days of wedding celebration and a tearful goodbye, Ebony and the king returned to their kingdom, leaving the happily married Snow White in the care of her husband.

Upon their return to the castle, the king's most trusted servant greeted them with a grave expression on his face and announced that the queen had died within her sleep this very morning.

"We didn't find any wounds or weapons," the servant assured the king. "It seems like she died naturally. There was nothing within her chamber that indicated any violence or poison. And the guards in front of her door didn't hear a thing."

The king instantly went to the chamber of his deceased wife, shortly followed by Ebony, who wanted to make sure that the queen was really dead. *She has been looking ill since the day she was convicted for the attempt of murder. Like she and her mirror had both been broken by her jealous wrath. But I didn't know that people could die from envy. Or did she sell her soul to the mirror to use its magic powers and now died like an empty shell due to its destruction?*

When she saw the stiff body and the lifeless cold eyes of the evil queen though, she was sure that not even this witch could have faked her own death. *Seems like this kingdom has lost a queen once again. I wonder if father will take this as a reason to marry me off even sooner than I thought, making me the future queen of his kingdom.*

She kept her thoughts to herself though and helped her father to prepare the funeral. Nobody was especially sad about the queen's death. The servants had feared and despised her for being rude and selfish all the time. Not even the king did seem too shocked by her death, though he did mourn for her for a short while.

"Do you think she had some kind of disease?" Ebony asked her father as they returned from the funeral. "Or could she have died of hatred? Envy?"

"I don't know," the king admitted honestly. "I'm not sure if envy can corrupt the heart in a way that is lethal. But I'm sure that she could have lived a long and happy life if she hadn't turned onto the path of evil."

Ebony nodded, deeply lost in thoughts.

The next few days were mostly spent in silence, while the king tended to his duties and the servants gave him space to mourn for his second wife.

There was not much sadness within Ebony's heart, even though she pitied the queen for having lost herself to the path of evil, which led to such an early death.

To turn her mind towards happier thoughts, she decided to write a letter to Viola, the only one whom she trusted enough to open up her heart and soul.

It took a few attempts and hours until Ebony was satisfied with what she'd written and once she had finished her letter, she read it out aloud to see whether it sounded appropriate.

"Dear Viola,

I hope that the journey back to your kingdom was pleasant and that this letter will find you happy and healthy. Since the day we have parted, I think of you a lot and cannot wait to meet you once again.

I would have written to you sooner, but things over here were a bit chaotic since the ball. I have ventured into the forest and actually found my sister, who had been poisoned by a witch, but was rescued and is now doing

180

well. It is a long story which I would rather tell you in person once we meet again.

Anyway, Snow White is married now and I fear that my father might want to marry me off soon, too. You see, my stepmother died a few days ago and now our kingdom is left without a queen. Thus, my father will definitely have no male heir – unless he decides to marry a third time, which I doubt – and will most likely want me to take over the throne. I never really wanted to be a queen, but I will do it if there is no other way.

Being a queen might not even be that bad, but there is something else that is bothering me. I do not dare to write it down in plain words in case anyone else reads this letter. But let me tell you this:

Ever since the day you left,
the stars are all I see.
They sparkle as bright as your eyes,
like a deep and calming sea.
With you by my side,
I could dance all night
or accomplish any task.
But we're far apart
and it aches my heart
to hide behind a mask."

Ebony paused, tears in her eyes. Her heart longed to write so much more, but she didn't dare to put any of her deeper feelings into words at that time. She quickly finished and signed the letter before she could change her mind about its content and sealed it with her signet ring.

She knew it would take a while until the letter would reach Viola in the south and even longer until her reply might arrive. To keep her mind busy in the meantime, she joined her father to witness his royal duties and get used to ruling a kingdom.

The king took this as a sign that Ebony was ready to meet her future duties as a queen and gladly explained to her the details of his decision-making.

"As a queen, it's important that you judge wisely and fair," the king often emphasised. "You have to open your mind for the view of others, look at the situation from their perspective. Like you witnessed with my late second wife, a story can have many different angles and versions. Mostly the truth is somewhere in between, so you have to look closely, but keep your eye at the bigger picture at the same time. Always stay open-minded and take your time."

"But what if a matter is urgent and a decision has to be made quickly?"

"You'll hopefully have enough practise by then, so that the lack of time won't cloud your mind and judgement. Just try to keep your mind open and look at every situation from different perspectives. Life is diverse and full of mystery. The truth might sometimes be hidden, but it can always be revealed by the true-hearted."

"So should I just trust my instincts when it comes to quick decisions?"

"If you have trained your instincts on finding the truth, then yes," the king agreed, happy about the cleverness of his daughter. "But you have to make sure that you stay focused on the truth. Otherwise, your mind might betray you and lead your instincts down a wrong path."

"But decisions of the heart can be wise, if the person is wise at heart, right?"

"Yes." The king smiled at Ebony with pride in his eyes. "And I'm sure that your heart will be the wisest and most true of them all. And kind. A good queen is also kind and lets mercy prevail where it is suited."

"How will I know when it is suited?"

"You will know," the king assured her calmly. "You have inherited your mother's loving and giving nature. Your kind heart will tell you when it's time for mercy."

Ebony couldn't help but feel a touch of doubt. *Can I really trust my heart? It has led me towards Snow White when I desperately wanted to find her, that's true. But it also longs for Viola – a love that is out of reach and maybe not even mutual.*

"You don't seem satisfied with my answer," the king remarked and watched Ebony intently. "Is there something else you'd like to know?"

"No – not really. I just wish there would be something a bit more specific to go by than 'trust your heart'. It doesn't seem like a reliable judge – at least not at all times."

"If you have faith in the truth and trust your own determination to find it, your heart and mind won't fail you. The truth is always stronger than lies and deception."

"But what if I'm not sure? What if my heart tells me something that is simply impossible? How do I know whether what I feel is the truth?"

"Skill comes with practice," the king replied and winked at her. "There is no shortcut in life. You have to train your mind, guide your heart and feelings. Human emotions are a fragile and fluttery thing, but when it comes to the cause of truth, our feelings are strong and invincible."

"You mean I'll be able to tell my own personal feelings apart from those which concern the general welfare?" Ebony pressed on with a doubtful frown. "Is there a difference between certain emotions?"

"Yes, you could say that. Personal feelings are very changeable. Whether you like a person or not might change over time or even during the cause of one conversation. But just like true love, the feeling of conviction and determination is stronger than other emotions."

Ebony's heart jumped at the mention of 'true love', but she quickly nodded and hoped that her father wouldn't notice her tension while he continued calmly.

"Once you know that something is the truth, neither your heart nor your mind will stray from their path of duty to protect it. You just have to give yourself some time and learn to trust in your heart and mind."

Ebony stared at her father, desperately trying to hide her emotions within a thankful smile. The mention of 'true love' had stirred her own feelings and she couldn't help but wonder if what she felt for Viola might be just that: true love. *If it is, my feelings won't change. No matter what father or anyone will say, I'll stay true to myself and find a way to live with Viola by my side – no matter what!*

Autumn had already advanced and the days gotten colder when Viola's letter finally arrived. Ebony's heart took a leap when she received it and couldn't wait to open it, but she restrained herself until she was alone in her chamber.

Her heart kept pounding furiously as she broke the seal with gentle hands and took a second to admire Viola's elegant handwriting. Then she started to read, absorbing every word, while she walked through the room to work off her excitement.

'Dear Ebony,

I gladly received your letter and your beautiful poem. It might have been short, but to me it speaks a thousand words and more. I can't wait to see you again and talk freely about everything.

Congratulations to your sister. I am glad that she could be saved and very proud of you for finding her. I can't wait to hear the full story behind all this!

Your father probably didn't tell you, but we were actually invited to Snow White's wedding. Due to the wedding of my older brother, which took place a few days later, we were unable to attend though. Otherwise, I would have loved to dance with you all night long – or maybe even for the rest of our lives?

And your father is not the only one who is thinking of marrying off his youngest daughter. My older sister has already been married for two years and now that my brother is married as well, my father's only concern is to marry me off, too.

I know winter is coming already, but do you think that we could see each other before the end of the year? I would love to invite you to our kingdom and show you everything we have talked about. Would you like to come and visit me?

I hope your father will approve of this. I can't leave right now, but maybe you will be able to visit me here in the south. It is still rather warm and I am sure you would like it here.

Until then I will think of you every day and look at the stars at night, remembering the depth of your wonderful dark eyes.

Hoping to see you soon!
Yours sincerely
Viola.'

Ebony stared at the words, which were becoming blurred due to the tears of joy welling up in her eyes. She noticed that she was actually holding her breath and inhaled deeply, before she read the letter once again, silently shaping the words with her lips and burning them into her mind. *She likes me! She would like to see me again soon and she's thinking of me as well. Could that mean that she's in love with me too?*

Her heart was celebrating that thought with a wild rhythm, letting the blood flush into her cheeks and making her head spin. *She liked the poem. Does she know what I was trying to tell her?*

After reading the letter for a third time, Ebony couldn't keep her excitement to herself anymore. She rushed into the throne room and surprised her father, who was just about to leave for the library.

"Ebony! My dear, what's the rush?"

"I received a letter from princess Viola today, father. And she invited us to her kingdom. Can we go? Please? She said it's still warm over there and she'd like to show me her kingdom and how their beautiful jewellery is made —"

"Hold your horses, young lady!" the king chuckled. "Winter is about to knock on our door very soon, remember? I'm not sure if it would be wise to leave right now. Without a queen, there is no one left to deal with my duties while I'm gone —"

"You could entrust that to your most reliable man and your counsellors, couldn't you? And it wouldn't have to be for long," Ebony pleaded. "We'd just like to — I would like to accept her invitation."

"But does it have to be this year?"

"Yes. Her brother got married recently and I'd like to congratulate them. And who knows — next year she might be busy with her own wedding preparations, if her father is as willing to marry her off as she suspects."

"Is he now?"

The king eyed his daughter closely, but she tried to hide her feelings as best as she could.

"You know," the king mused, "you've never been an open book — very unlike your sister or mother. I can't tell why, but for some reason this seems to be very important to you. Would you let me know me why?"

Ebony couldn't help it. She blushed and had to put every ounce of will into keeping eye contact with her father. *If I look away now, he'll know that something is the matter. That would be even worse than blushing.*

"I just think that it would be appropriate to accept the invitation as soon as possible, before princess Viola might be tied up with other matters," Ebony stated as calmly as possible. "And winter is still a few weeks off. I don't see why weather should be a problem."

"Well, I have to admit that your arguments sound reasonable enough." The king smiled fondly. "I guess the kingdom should be able to manage without us for a short while. It'll take us a few days to travel down to the south though. So you'd better tell princess Viola that we won't be staying long."

"Thank you!"

Ebony threw herself into her father's arms and hugged him tightly. He was taken by surprise by this sudden outburst of emotion, but hugged her back, before she ran off again to write back to Viola.

Due to the approaching winter, they didn't wait for Viola's reply and just started their preparations for the voyage right away.

The king insisted that Ebony would help him to ensure that the kingdom was safe and well cared for, so that she had to spend hours and hours of council meetings with the king's most trusted men.

Why are there no women among the council anyway? she thought to herself, while listening to another discussion between the king and his counsellors. *It would be nice to hear an empathetic point of view once in a while.*

After one week of preparation, the courier – which Ebony had sent to Viola with the urgent plea for a quick answer – returned with a short letter, stating that Viola and her parents would be delighted to welcome Ebony and her father into their kingdom as soon as they could come.

They decided to set out right on the next morning, hoping to be on their way home again before winter arrived in full.

Ebony spent the night lying awake, staring at the starry sky and imagining what she might say to Viola once they were finally able to talk freely. *Should I just tell her that I love her right away? Or should I wait to see how she feels? But we'll only be staying with them for a few days ... If I wait, I might miss my chance to open up my heart to her. But what if she doesn't return my feelings? Maybe she only likes me as a good friend. I might ruin that friendship if I actually ask her to marry me. And even if she says yes – would it be possible for us to get married? Would our parents accept our love or try to talk us out of it?*

Too many questions without answers spiralled through her sleepless mind and kept Ebony awake until the first glow of sunrise illuminated the sky. *Two days of journey. That's all I've got to decide what I'm going to do. I just hope that father won't mind if I'm lost in thoughts all the time.*

𝕰𝖇𝖔𝖓𝖞 wasn't the only one who was eager to travel to the south. The king actually loved to go there and it was a special occasion for him to take one of his daughters to this fair and distant kingdom.

The two days passed in a rush of excitement, while Ebony stared blankly at the changing landscape, trying to find answers to her unsolvable questions.

Luckily the king didn't notice her mind's absence. He was too happy to spend some time with his daughter and told her everything about his recent travels to the south, not minding his silent listener.

Sometimes Ebony actually paid attention to his stories to distract herself from her growing anxiety. She asked questions about the different animals and plants they saw from the windows of their carriage, which seemed to increase in colour and beauty the more they journeyed south.

There were still a lot of flowers in full bloom, unaware of the upcoming winter, dotting the landscape with lush reds, greens and yellows. Even the earth seemed a little reddish, while the leaves of the trees were of a bright green, seeming to glow in the warm sunlight which shone down on them as if winter was still months away.

"How cold does it get in winter down here in the south?" Ebony asked the king as they crossed over a broad river. "Lady Viola said that they don't get much snow."

"That's true. It doesn't get as cold as it gets in the north. The nights can be quite icy though, so you should stay indoors after nightfall. But there won't be any snow while we're here. They only get snow in the deep of winter."

"So they have no frozen lakes to play on?"

The king eyed his daughter with furrowed brows before he answered her.

"I don't think so. Normally it doesn't get *that* cold around here. But you shouldn't walk on frozen lakes anyway. It is way too dangerous!"

Ebony just nodded and turned her gaze towards the window again, closing her eyes and bathing her face in the pleasant sunlight.

On the third day, just as the sun was climbing up to the peak of her ascent, they finally drew close to the small castle which was Viola's home. Ebony clung to the frame of her window and couldn't take her eyes off the elegant building, which was rising like a giant sand statue out of the lush greenery around it.

"It looks like it's made of sand!" she exclaimed, while she eyed the high windows and short towers.

"It is," the king replied with a smile on his face. "It's a special kind of sandstone. Only here in the south they know how to treat it to become as sturdy as that castle."

"How old is it?"

"Older than ours, that's for sure."

"Wow!"

Ebony gaped at the castle as they approached it, but soon her attention was directed towards the small ring of villages which surrounded the castle area. When they came closer, she spotted a few houses which were also built of sand, but most of the newer ones seemed to be made out of regular stone, even though they had a reddish colour to them.

"Why is everything red around here?"

"It's the soil," the king explained wisely. "There is something in the earth that makes it look red. And the buildings get covered in the dust during sand storms, making them appear red as well."

"Sand storms? But I thought those would only occur in a desert. It's rather green and lush around here."

"True. But don't be fooled. The desert is not as far off as you might think. Look."

The king pointed to a point near the horizon. Ebony could only make out a lot of reddish looking landscape, like a line of glowing soil. The air seemed to shimmer, but Ebony wasn't sure if that wasn't just a trick of her eyes.

"That's the desert then? The reddish part back there?"

The king nodded.

"Yes. It stays rather hot in the desert, even during early winter. But the nights get cold and icy, so you should never travel there unprepared."

"Sounds ridiculous to bring enough warm clothes to the desert," Ebony said chuckling.

"Don't be fooled. You should always wear the right clothes – night and day. If you'd walk around with short sleeves during the day, you would risk a serious sun burn. You should always wear long clothes in the desert to protect yourself from the heat. Especially you, with your fair skin. You would turn as red as your hair in a matter of minutes, I'm sure."

Ebony shrugged and turned her gaze back towards the castle, which was towering in front of them now.

"I'll keep it in mind. But we won't have the time to visit the desert anyway, will we?"

"I don't think so. I would rather not stay longer than two days before we head back. The kingdom is still dealing with the loss of its second queen and I don't like being away for too long."

Ebony sighed, but nodded. *Guess I'll have to be straight forward about my feelings then. I just hope that Viola feels the same way …*

There was no time to let the panic settle within her heart, as they arrived at the castle soon after.

Viola and her parents greeted them in the courtyard, accompanied by a bunch of servants who tried hard to provide some shade with a few parasols.

"Lady Ebony!" Viola exclaimed with a beaming smile on her face. "It's a pleasure to welcome you in our kingdom."

"The pleasure is all mine," Ebony replied with a small curtsy. "Thank you very much for your kind invitation."

After greeting Viola's parents, the grown-ups soon adjourned into the inside of the castle, while Viola insisted on showing Ebony around the gardens.

"I'm so glad you came," she sighed and took Ebony by surprise by giving her a tight hug. "My heart yearned for your presence since I've read your poem. I couldn't bear to think about giving in to father's wish to marry me off before we had had a chance to talk to each other."

She let go of Ebony and looked into her eyes with an expression of longing and passion on her tanned face. Ebony's heart started to race, fluttering inside her chest like a scared bird. *Does this mean that she loves me too?*

"I – I'm glad that you – liked the poem," she mumbled, too overwhelmed by the sudden rush of emotions to find the right words.

"I loved it," Viola breathed, moving closer so that Ebony could smell the soft scent of flowers and sand that seemed to surround her. "I have written a poem in return, but I didn't dare to send it to you. Would you like to read it now?"

Ebony nodded, not able to speak a single word.

Viola dragged Ebony behind a tall ornamental bush and reached into the décolleté neckline of her peach-coloured dress. Ebony held her breath, following Viola's lean fingers with her eyes. The blood rushed into her cheeks as she imagined her own fingertips gliding down the soft curves, which were just visible within the décolleté.

As Viola took out a folded piece of parchment, Ebony's heart took a flying leap and a rush of excitement made her head feel dizzy. She had to take a deep breath to keep her hands from trembling as she took the small piece of parchment and unfolded it.

'My mind is like a sea
filled with thoughts of you.
Your face is all I see.
Oh, make my wish come true!
My heart longs for your touch,
my eyes yearn for thine.
To let you go would be too much,
you are too divine.
I need you by my side,
now and forever.
If you would be my bride,
I could brave the weather.
Any storm or danger
would seem like silly trouble.
No mortal earthly anger
could divide us as a couple.'

The elegantly curved letters became blurred as Ebony's eyes started to fill with tears of joy. She read the poem a second time, blinking away the salty traitors, while her heart was about to burst from her chest.

When she finally dared to look up again, Viola had come so close that her deep brown eyes were all she could see, leaving her speechless once again.

Viola lifted up her left hand and gently brushed away the tears from Ebony's cheeks. Her fingertips sent a pleasant shudder down Ebony's spine, igniting the insides of her lower belly as if a swarm of fireflies had been set free inside her.

"I know that we haven't known each other for long," Viola broke the silence with a soft voice, "but I can't imagine to marry anyone else. Father is not giving me much of a choice in the matter of time, so I have to rush things a bit. If that should be too much for you – or you don't feel the same way –"

"I do," Ebony breathed.

"You do?"

"Yes. I mean – no. It's not too much – or too soon. And I definitely feel the same way! As a matter of fact, I was kind of planning to ask you the same question –"

"Really?"

Viola's face lightened up like a summer's morning and Ebony beamed right back at her.

"Yes," she said with fervour. "Viola – I – I love you."

Tears of joy welled up in the dark brown eyes in front of her. Then Viola threw herself into Ebony's arms and kissed her passionately.

"I love you too," she whispered into her ear before her lips found Ebony's once more.

Jolts of lust and delight sped through Ebony's body. She pressed Viola's warm face against hers, pulling her into a tight hug, while her fingers were gripping Viola's waist and hair with growing excitement.

Viola's fingertips were caressing her cheeks, her eyebrows, moving through her red hair and down her neck, leaving a trace of goose bumps behind them.

A soft moan of pleasure escaped Ebony's lips as Viola let her left hand wander down Ebony's spine, tracing the curves of her butt.

Ebony let her own hand glide up from Viola's waist, until she reached the edge of the peach-coloured décolleté. Viola gasped as Ebony touched her skin, tracing the curves of Viola's breasts and letting her hand rest right above her heart, which was beating just as furiously as Ebony's.

Viola pulled back her face and eyed Ebony with fiery eyes while she placed her own hand above Ebony's heart.

"Will you marry me?" she asked in a low voice, taking Ebony's face into her other hand.

"Yes," Ebony mouthed, tears in her eyes. "I want to be by your side, now and forever. I love you. And I always will."

Astonished faces stared back at Ebony and Viola, who were standing hand in hand within the small throne room of the sand castle.

Ebony couldn't believe that Viola had actually worked up the courage to go straight to her parents just minutes after their proposal. She herself barely managed to return her father's shocked gaze, let alone open her mouth to explain herself.

"This is a joke, isn't it?" he asked with a plea in his voice, looking back and forth between his daughter and Viola.

"No, not at all," the princess of the south answered with a firm voice, gently squeezing Ebony's hand to encourage her to say something.

"I – We," Ebony stuttered, "we – we love each other."

"For Heaven's sake! Ebony, listen to yourself. This is ridiculous! You are the future queen of our northly kingdom. You can't just run off, marrying a *woman* – love at first sight or not."

"But why not? Mother told me to listen to my heart in matters of love. 'Choose your own destiny' she always said. Well, I have. I chose Viola. And she's a princess too."

"Yes, but she's a *woman*, Ebony. No offense, lady Viola. But this is just not possible."

The king turned towards Viola's parents, who seemed too confused to speak yet.

"I don't mean to be rude," Viola replied sternly, "but I don't see why my sex should be a problem in this matter. It may not be common for two women or men to love each other, but that's no reason to forbid our love."

"That's not the point," the king replied sternly. "You can love each other all you want. But marriage? I don't have a son who can secure my bloodline. Ebony was supposed to

197

take the throne and marry a worthy man with whom she could reign my kingdom –"

"Well, I'm not a man," Viola softly interrupted the king, "but I think I'd be worthy still. I am of royal blood and know just as much about ruling a kingdom as my brother. I would be by Ebony's side to help her, as loyal and faithful as any husband could be."

"But you won't be able to get children," the king sighed as if the mere thought was torturing him. "What about our bloodline? How will you produce an heir who can inherit the throne?"

Silence filled the room. Viola pressed her lips together, apparently lost for words. Ebony took a deep breath to summon her courage and finally turned to her father to speak up too.

"Do we have to have children? Couldn't we just choose a worthy heir? Adopt a child? Or let the people choose a successor for the throne before we die?"

"The people?" her father exclaimed. "How would the people choose someone? And whom could they choose? A prince from another country?"

"Why not one of the members of the royal council?" Ebony offered firmly. "I'm sure there would be a way to find someone worthy who could be trusted with the throne."

They both went quiet, while Viola's parents found their voices again and turned towards their daughter.

"You really mean it then?" the king of the south asked with surprise in his voice. "You want to marry lady Ebony?"

"Yes, father," Viola stated with a happy voice. "I do."

"But," the queen asked quickly, "do you truly love each other? You've only known lady Ebony for a very short time. Are you sure about this?"

"Yes, I am. We both are."

Viola darted a glance at Ebony who nodded in return.

"Yes," she confirmed Viola's statement. "We love each other and want to spend the rest of our lives together. I couldn't think of anyone else who would be better suited to rule the north kingdom with me. I'm sure Viola would make a worthy and splendid queen. That's why I humbly ask you for her hand in marriage and would be honoured to receive your blessing."

Ebony tried her best to meet the gaze of Viola's parents. To her relief, the queen of the south smiled fondly as she looked at the two young women in front of her.

"Yes," she answered. "I can see that your love for each other is genuine. You have my blessing if your own father will consent to this matter."

Ebony sighed in relief and returned the queen's kind smile, before turning back to her father. It was the king of the south though who spoke next, drawing her attention to himself.

"I don't know about this. My son is already married and thus my own bloodline is secure. But I'm not sure how the people will react when they hear that Viola will be married to a woman. It's not common for members of the royal family —"

"But for other people," Viola exclaimed and furrowed her brows in an angry manner. "We have finally achieved an acceptance for homosexual relationships within the south over the last years. Why would there be any difference just because I'm a princess?"

"First of all, you have more responsibilities than common folks," the king of the south lectured her seriously. "And secondly, it is true that the love between men or the relationships between women are tolerated in the south, but none of them are married."

"So *marriage* is the problem?" Viola snorted in disbelief. "We would be allowed to love each other, but can't be married?"

"It's just unheard of! Marriage does involve the heritage of a bloodline. It's a matter of securing your family name and producing an heir to do so. How on earth would you do that? You can't just *choose* someone to inherit your name and blood."

"Is it really that important to uphold our bloodline? Or our family name? Does that matter? Shouldn't things like love, kindness, friendship and loyalty matter more than the stupid bloodline?"

"Easy for you to say," the king of the south sighed. "Your brother is already doing the job for you and securing our bloodline."

"Oh, come on!" Viola burst out. "I can't hear it anymore. Who cares about this? Won't future generations be happier if they live in a world of peace and love, instead of a world of pure bloodlines?"

"This is not your decision to make," Viola's father replied sternly and looked towards his friend. "It is not our kingdom. We should let lady Ebony and her father decide what's best for his kingdom."

All eyes turned towards the king of the north, who had furrowed his brow so deeply that it looked like the bark of an ancient tree.

"Lady Viola has a point," he said slowly. "Love and loyalty should be important for a ruler, just as much as kindness and justice. But I don't think that it would be wise to confront our people with such a drastic change. It is strange enough that Ebony will be the future queen, because I don't have a son to fill that spot. But putting a princess by her side instead of a man – I don't think that the people would approve of this."

"How can you be so sure?" Ebony fired back. "Maybe the people wouldn't even care as long as they have a kind ruler. We could just ask them."

"No, we couldn't! What if they disagree with you? What if they don't approve? You can't take back a thing like that. Once you've told them about the way you feel, they will always perceive you as a woman who loves a woman. You won't be able to change your mind and marry a prince instead, if you've asked them this question first."

"I won't change my mind about this," Ebony squeezed out between gritted teeth. "Either the people agree with my choice or I renounce the throne. I don't want to be the future queen if I can't have Viola by my side."

The king gasped and stared at his daughter with shock on his face.

"You can't just renounce the throne, Ebony. You are the future queen!"

"Well, in that case I should be able to make my own decision and rules. And one of those will be to enable any couple – may they be of the same sex or not – to marry each other. If true love would bond them together anyway, I don't see a reason to not allow them to marry. Viola and I will be the best example of that."

"And what if I don't allow it? I'm still the king and you are not yet a queen."

"Then I won't marry until I'm able to choose my partner myself. I'm in no hurry to be a queen anyway."

"I could force you to marry a prince."

"No, father." Ebony met the king's gaze with grim determination. "You couldn't and you won't."

They stared at each other for a long time, while no one dared to speak a word. Viola grasped Ebony's hand even tighter as if to make sure that the king wouldn't just rip their fingers apart.

"You were always the stubborn one," the king finally mumbled. "Why couldn't you just be like your sister? She never caused me any trouble."

"You mean except when she disappeared and nearly died, right?" Ebony retorted with a bitter voice. "Who was the one to go after her and try to save her? Who found out about the evil witch who called herself queen? Who saved the kingdom from her envious wrath?"

"This is not –"

"Oh, this is *exactly* the point!" Ebony exclaimed bitterly. "You're never satisfied, no matter what I achieve. I've never been good enough for you. Snow White was always the perfect one, while I was merely a nuisance. And now that she's happily married, you want to turn me into another version of her."

"That's not true. I've always loved you both."

"Sure. But you only paid attention to me after mother's death. And even then, you still preferred Snow White's company. I was too gloomy, too witty, too skinny, too boyish, too pale, too dark-eyed, too red-haired – admit it: I'm just not the kind of daughter you wished for."

"That's enough!" the king commanded with a booming voice. "This is neither the time nor the place to discuss matters like this. Have you forgotten your manners?!"

"Oh, right. Another thing I'm not good at: manners. I've never been as cute or sweet as Snow White, have I?"

"This is not about your sister –"

"What is it about then? *You* were the one to mention her first, not me. You said I should be more like her, should

202

be less troublesome. Well, I'm not her! I never will be. And I don't want to be! I'm me – and if that isn't enough for you, then you shouldn't choose me as the future queen for your kingdom anyway!"

"Well, maybe you're right," the king answered with an angry growl. "You definitely don't act like one right now! No queen should be as childish and selfish as you. All you can think about are your own emotions. But what about the people? Is your love more important than their well-being? Shouldn't you put their needs over yours?"

"I *do* care about the people. I just don't think that they would object against my marriage with Viola."

"And what if they do object?" the king challenged her with a cold voice. "Will you run away and leave the kingdom without an heir?"

"Why not? Apparently, you don't think that I'm suited to be the queen anyway. You should choose one of your most trusted *men* to do the job if you're so proud of the male sex. Or maybe Snow White will give birth to a son one day, who could take over our kingdom. Or you marry again and try to get a son of your own who can finally satisfy your need for a male heir."

"Don't be foolish," the king chided her. "You are acting very disrespectful. What is the matter with you?"

"Me? What's the matter with *me?* I'm not the one trying to ruin a perfectly happy engagement."

"You two are *not* engaged! I won't allow it."

"Fine!" Ebony hissed. "Then I resign! Maybe you're lucky and you'll manage to produce a male heir before you're too old."

With that she spun round on her heel and stormed out of the throne room, dragging a very bewildered Viola behind her.

𝔅𝔩𝔞𝔷𝔦𝔫𝔤 heat made Ebony's head feel dizzy. It scorched her thoughts, turned them into dust, which was carried away by the hot breeze.

"We should turn back."

Viola's worried voice drifted through the air like the red sand, which filled their sight and stretched towards the horizon like a never-ending sea.

"No," Ebony panted, shielding her eyes and staring out into the red desert. "I'm not going back."

"But this is foolish! We don't have any warm clothes with us and not enough water to last for more than a day. It would be suicide to stay out here for the night, let alone the next day."

"Are there no lakes or rivers?"

"Not in the desert. Only underground springs, but they will be hard to find."

"Can't the horses sniff them out?"

"We might try, but we would probably die before we find something."

"Gosh," Ebony sighed playfully. "Couldn't you say something encouraging for a change?"

Viola chuckled and let her horse ride next to Ebony's to grasp her hand, which was already feeling raw and withered.

"There is a legend about a southern princess who fell in love with an ordinary peasant. They ran away into the desert, because they couldn't bear to be apart. For two days and nights they wandered through the red sand, until they suddenly found an oasis. There was plenty of water, which sprang from the ground and palms which provided shade and food. The two stayed there and –"

"– lived happily ever after?"

"Something like that. I was going to say 'and had lots of cute children', but I guess that's not much of an option for us anyway."

They both snickered.

"I don't even want children," Ebony mumbled, bringing her horse to a standstill and surveying the bleak area. "Do you? I never really liked the idea of having little redheads driving me crazy –"

"Oh, I'm sure they would be adorable," Viola said with a smile. "But I think I could manage without them. You on the other hand I wouldn't want to miss in my life ever again. And that's why we should turn back now. Your skin doesn't look too good."

Ebony let her gaze drop down towards her arms, which were only poorly covered by a thin silk scarf that Viola had given her to protect herself from the sun.

"I admit that my skin is burning a little," Ebony grumbled. "And my head feels like the water is evaporating right out of my skull."

Viola eyed her with worry on her face and handed her the waterskin, which the stable master had given to them when they had fled the castle in a rush.

Ebony gulped down some of the warm water, closing her eyes to try and gather her thoughts.

"Sorry," she said as she handed back the waterskin to Viola. "It was stupid to run off like this. I just – I couldn't stand it anymore. I had to get away for a bit –"

"I understand."

Viola took a few sips of water herself, before she turned around her horse and held her hand out towards Ebony.

"Let's get back. You start to look like a tomato and I would never forgive myself if I lost my fiancé to the forces of nature out here in the desert."

Ebony smiled and made her horse turn around as well to ride by Viola's side. Hand in hand, they made their way back towards the villages and the castle, which was illuminated by the setting sun.

"It looks like the sand is on fire," Ebony whispered awestruck, eyeing the spectacle of nature with humble admiration.

"Beautiful, isn't it?" Viola agreed, watching the sun turn the castle into a glowing mass of sand. "I always loved to watch the sun set, especially since it reminded me of your beautiful hair."

She winked at Ebony, who couldn't help but let out a frustrated snort.

"Beautiful? People called my red hair a lot of things, but 'beauty' was never involved in them. I've always wondered how I turned out to be a redhead anyway. Neither my mother nor father have red hair. Some of the servants even believed that I wasn't truly the king's child."

"That's nonsense. You and Snow White are twins, aren't you? You were born in the same night. How could you not be the king's daughter?"

"I don't know," Ebony sighed, watching the shades grow longer. "I just feel like my whole existence is a big mistake. Like I wasn't supposed to be here."

"No way!" Viola exclaimed emphatically. "You are the best thing that ever happened to me. If it weren't for you, I'd never have found my true love."

"Maybe you would have fallen in love with someone else – someone with whom your parents could agree."

"My mother already gave us her blessing! And my father is only holding back, because he is afraid of change. And of the anger of your father. He doesn't want to betray his trust. The two of them have been friends for years."

"Yes, I know. But it is so unfair!" Ebony whined frustrated. "Why would our sex be of importance when it comes to true love? Shouldn't they be happy for us?"

"I'm sure they are. They just don't know it yet, because it is all too new and weird for them. But they'll get used to it after a while."

"I don't know." Ebony shook her head as she thought of her father's angry eyes. "My father didn't seem too willing to give us his blessing. He wouldn't even accept our engagement –"

"He will. We just have to stay strong and show him that we deserve his trust."

Viola gave Ebony an encouraging smile and squeezed her hand. *I really hope that she's right. Because if father shouldn't give in – I don't know what I'll do. I couldn't survive a life as the queen without Viola by my side. And I definitely couldn't marry a prince just to make father proud. He should be proud of me the way I am.*

While Ebony and Viola returned to the castle with the last light of the day, the young fairy apprentice turned away from the mirror she had been staring at for the last few hours.

"Is it true?" she asked quietly, looking up at the Good Fairy, who was sitting in her armchair with closed eyes. "Is Ebony's existence just a stupid mistake? Am I responsible for her misery?"

"No, my dear," the Good Fairy responded soothingly. "There are no mistakes when it comes to fate. Whatever it was good for, this little mistake of yours was supposed to happen."

"Ebony didn't choose that destiny though," Arabella sighed heavily. "It's all my fault. Why does life have to be so hard on her?"

"She chose her path in life herself and thus her fate is sealed, even though it might seem unfair sometimes."

"You mean that she did kind of choose her destiny herself by the decisions she made?"

"Exactly."

"But why is Ebony having so much trouble then?"

"Maybe it is her destiny to be in trouble," the old fairy mused, rocking back and forth in her armchair. "It may seem to you like she wasn't supposed to exist in the first place, but don't be fooled. See how much good she has done already. She has saved the kingdom of the evil queen. Who knows whom else this witch would have killed if anyone would have had the bad luck to be fairer than her?"

"It's not like I'm not proud of Ebony," the young fairy mumbled. "But does she have to suffer so much?"

"Some people are destined to suffer, because it makes them stronger. Those who have a difficult life know how to endure and how to fight for justice. It might be the only way to prepare Ebony for the challenges of her life as a queen."

Arabella nodded, but stayed silent while she turned back towards the mirror. She didn't like to admit it, but the words of the Good Fairy made sense in a weird way. And even though she would have loved to see Ebony happy again, she was sure that all the hardship had to be worth something.

"I hope you stay strong once more," she whispered while she watched Ebony and Viola returning to the throne room. She laid her hand upon the cold glass of the mirror as if to caress Ebony's shoulder and smiled fondly.

"You deserve a joyful life and I'm sure that you'll find it if you follow your dreams. And who knows – your love might even change the world."

𝕿𝖍𝖊 king was glad to see Ebony return, but he was also furious about her leaving the castle area in the first place. While Viola stayed in the throne room with her own parents, the king ordered Ebony to follow him into a private chamber so that they could have a talk from father to daughter one-on-one.

"It was absolutely reckless to leave the castle," he grunted once they were alone. "Especially that late in the evening! I wouldn't have thought that you might be so irresponsible. Why do you keep running away? Didn't I tell you *not* to go to the desert? It was stupid and childish. That's not how a future queen should behave."

"I know," Ebony said quietly while she forced herself to remain calm. "I'm sorry for acting so stubborn. But if you would have listened to me earlier –"

"There was nothing to listen to."

"See?!" Ebony moaned in exasperation. "You're not even listening to me now! You are too busy worrying about everything – how people think about me, how they might react if they find out about my love for Viola, how I will behave as a queen, about your bloodline … The only thing you can do is worry and make me feel miserable for mistakes I haven't even made yet."

The king stared at her smitten with surprise. Ebony returned his gaze with a face of steel, hoping that she sounded serious rather than furious.

"Well," the king replied after a while, "it is the duty of a father to worry about his children. I just want to keep you safe and protect you."

"Protect me from what? From making mistakes? It's *important* to make mistakes. They help us learn and grow by ourselves instead of just watching others live their life. I want to choose my own destiny."

"You can – you always have, actually. You were way too stubborn to protect you from harm all the time. And you seem to love driving me crazy by doing all kinds of risky things and placing yourself in danger."

"Other people call it *living* and being curious."

"Curious?" The king snorted. "I'd call it nosy beyond reason. Another matter why I always have to worry about you. Being nosy brings only trouble –"

"No, it brings knowledge and experience," Ebony argued confidently. "And I don't agree about you having to worry all the time. It's not just the duty of a father to worry about his children. You should be proud of us as well – love us – encourage us to live our own life –"

"I definitely want you to be happy and I am proud of you all the time. But do you have to live your life with Viola as your wife? Does it have to be that way?"

"Why not?" Ebony argued passionately. "Just because it's never been done before doesn't mean that it's not good. There is a first time for everything."

"Maybe there are things which are not meant to be," the king pointed out sternly. "What if there isn't supposed to be a first time in this case?"

"Then I wouldn't understand why fate made it possible for me to fall in love with Viola in the first place. It would seem awfully cruel to let love grow where it cannot bloom."

"It might have been a mistake –"

"Seriously? You call our love a mistake??"

"Well, you never know. Nature makes mistakes sometimes. Maybe you only misunderstood your feelings for Viola, because you wished for a friend so dearly that you thought it was love."

Now it was Ebony's turn to stare at her father with wide eyes. Her mouth stood half-open, but there were no words to express her feelings at that moment.

The king mistook her speechlessness for agreement and dared to pursue his train of thought a bit more.

"I know that you've been lonely sometimes and I'm very sorry that it was so difficult for you to find friends. It was not fair that most people didn't like you due to your appearance, but that is no reason to fall in love with the first available person who does not make fun of your hair."

"Viola is NOT just a 'first available person'!" Ebony exploded. "She is the love of my life! She understands me and loves me for who I am. She doesn't care about my red hair – she even thinks that it looks beautiful! And we have so much in common –"

"Which might make her a good friend, but not a good wife. It's not natural –"

"Then why does nature allow it?" Ebony hissed. "Why is it possible for women and men to fall in love with their own sex, if nature doesn't want it? If it were only my case, I'd say that it might be a mistake. But I'm not the only one. And nature doesn't make that many mistakes, does it?"

"Who knows? I haven't heard of that many cases where women fell in love with each other – or men with men. You might just assume that –"

"I'm not assuming anything! I know this. Viola told me about people in the villages here and how they finally accept this kind of relationships. There are not just two or three of us. And the acceptance of the people around here shows that it can be possible for us to live together. Viola and I would just be the first ones to marry, that's all."

"It's still a huge change," the king argued. "How can you assume that the people would agree to your marriage?

How will you explain to them that you won't have children? No heir for the throne?"

"Do we have to talk about *that* again?" Ebony sighed annoyed and rolled her eyes. "We could just adopt children or vote for an heir or wait for Snow White to bear one. We might choose a trusted person before we die or let the people decide whom they want as our successor. There are lots of possibilities to ensure that the throne won't stay empty."

Ebony paused and held her breath, while she watched her father ponder on her words. He had furrowed his brow so deeply that it looked like a landscape of hills, with the dark lakes of his doubtful eyes at their bottom.

"Fine," he finally agreed and eyed his daughter with grim concern. "I will give you my blessing, if the people of our kingdom choose to accept your decision. You will tell them yourself about the engagement with Viola. But if only one person doesn't agree to be ruled by a queen who is married to a woman, you will break off the engagement and marry someone more suitable."

Ebony gritted her teeth to keep herself from arguing about that last sentence. *Viola is the most suitable person for this position that I know! It is not fair to regard her as unsuitable just because she is a woman.*

Instead of starting another discussion, Ebony met the gaze of her father with stern determination.

"I agree to tell the people of our kingdom about my engagement and will see to it that all opinions shall be heard. But first you will apologise to Viola for your rudeness and officially accept our engagement."

"Agreed."

The king gave her a short nod and for a second she thought that he might actually be a little proud of her for standing her ground. *He'll see that there is nothing to worry about. I just have to make sure that everybody in our kingdom is happy with the choice I've made.*

*

Ebony was truly relieved when Viola had accepted her father's apology – just as happy as Viola's parents were when they heard that the king was giving his official blessing for the engagement.

"I'm sure the people in your kingdom will see the truth of your love," Viola's mother assured Ebony before they said their good-byes. "Just make sure that you stay true to yourself and let no one tell you how you're supposed to feel. Your heart is the only one who can tell you that."

After the first relief subsided, Ebony was troubled by agonising anxiety again, refusing to speak to her father at all while they travelled back home.

While staring out of the window most of the time, she constantly saw Viola's face in front of her mind's eye. The look of encouragement she gave her when they parted. And the sparkle of hope within those beautiful dark eyes, which amplified her wish to succeed at her task. *I have to persuade the people of the righteousness of our marriage. Or maybe they'll just accept it if I can make them see that our love is true and honest. But will they believe me?*

Doubts kept creeping into her thoughts from the back of her mind, but she pushed them back with all the power her will could muster. *True love always wins. Otherwise, it wouldn't be true love – right?*

Ⱦⱨℯ Good Fairy didn't look happy at all, while she strode up and down the Chamber of Sight at an unusually brisk pace. Her brows were furrowed so deeply that they reminded the young fairy of a rutted mountainside, her forehead a dark thundercloud, hovering over the flashing storm in the grey old eyes.

"This could be a disaster," she grumbled, flinging her arms into the air. "I should have seen this coming!"

"Um," the young fairy quietly interrupted the furious outburst. "I don't understand. *What* might be a disaster?"

"The wedding, of course," the Good Fairy spit out with so much dislike that her apprentice almost didn't recognise her good-natured mistress anymore. "If Ebony should actually succeed ... The masses always love a good story about true love and all that. They might accept her choice and let her marry that – that –"

"Princess Viola?"

"Exactly!"

"But," Arabella stammered baffled, "I thought that you were on Ebony's side. Didn't you want for her to become queen?"

"Oh, she may be a queen one day, alright. But not one married to a woman!"

"I don't understand –"

"Because you're young and foolish, just like princess Ebony," grunted the Good Fairy and sunk into her armchair. "You believe that true love is all that counts. But I tell you, it doesn't."

"Why not? What is so wrong about Ebony marrying Viola? I think they would make two wonderful queens and guide the kingdom into a new age of –"

"Nonsense!" the Good Fairy hushed her strictly. "This kingdom isn't ready for such foolishness. They are women! How would they lead an army if there should be a war? Do you think true love can solve all problems?"

"No, but you said yourself that Ebony has such a hard time so that she can get stronger. You said that destiny wants to prepare her for the challenges of being a queen. Doesn't that include warfare?"

"Pshaw!" the Good Fairy exclaimed with contempt. "Just because women sometimes have to fight in battles as well, doesn't mean that they are fit to *lead* an army!"

"Well, maybe Ebony will be the first queen to do so then," Arabella retorted sulkily. "There's a first time for everything."

The Good Fairy just shook her head and stared gloomily at the image of Ebony and her father, returning to their own castle in silence.

"But you won't interfere, right?" her apprentice asked quietly, looking back and forth between Ebony and her mistress.

"No. Even though I'm tempted to do so. But that's not what we fairies do. We grant wishes and sometimes help the humans a little by guiding them towards the right path, but that's it. Destiny will take care of the rest."

The young fairy sighed with relief and turned her gaze back upon Ebony with a new glimmer of hope in it.

"I'm sure destiny has great plans for you," she mouthed silently and smiled fondly at the image in the mirror. "No matter what happens, things will fall into place. Because true love should always win. And I will watch over you."

Ebony had persuaded her father to give her three days to prepare for the task at hand: Convincing the people of their kingdom to let her marry Viola because of true love.

Time seemed to have sped up though and the days just flashed past, hours turning into seconds and minutes vanishing into thin air, while Ebony paced up and down her room, getting more nervous with every step she took.

Her father left her to herself, only coming to her room to remind her to eat once in a while.

"Starvation is the least of my problems right now," she mumbled, following him into the dining hall. "I still have no idea how I am even supposed to start my speech."

"Would you like for me to do the introduction?", the king offered knowingly and tried to give her an encouraging smile. "Maybe it will be easier if I address the people first and you take over after a few minutes."

"I would like that," Ebony sighed in relief and returned the smile, before piling food on her plate as if she hadn't eaten in days. "Thank you, father."

"You are always welcome, my dear."

Filled by new hope, Ebony didn't return to her chamber later on, but went into the kitchen instead and asked the servants for their opinion.

She had decided that, if she really wanted for the people to accept her, she needed to understand their point of view first, before deciding how to address the masses.

"You want to marry *a woman*, my lady?!" was the most common answer, which didn't surprise her much.

The cook nearly let a spoon fall into the soup, while Ebony's maiden stared at her with an open mouth for a second, before remembering her manners and quickly apologising for her behaviour.

"It's alright," Ebony assured all of them. "I just want to know whether or not you would accept my choice and still want me as your queen?"

"Of course, my lady," her maiden replied, quickly lowering her eyes. "It is your decision, not mine."

"Yes, but if it *were* your decision, what would *you* do?"

The maiden blushed and lowered her head a little more.

"I don't know, my lady."

"Wouldn't you want to marry because of love?"

"Of course, my lady."

"So if your choice would be to either marry the one you love or someone you don't even like, which one would you choose?"

"The one I love, I guess, my lady."

"And would you still accept me and want me as your queen if I would do the same?"

"Yes, my lady."

Ebony sighed and tried to force a smile upon her face.

"Look at me," she said with a soft voice.

The maiden looked up, but Ebony noticed how her fingers started to tremble a little.

"It's alright," she assured the woman who was barely older than herself. "Just look me in the eye and tell me what you *really* think. No matter what it is. Just be honest."

"I – I – don't –"

"No matter what you say, I'm not going to be mad at you or punish you. I just want to hear your opinion. Please? Do it as a favour for me, yes?"

"My lady, I don't know – this is a big decision – I could never – I –"

"What would you do if you were in my place?"

"Run away?" the maiden suggested, blushing even more. "So that you don't have to make such a hard decision?"

"And leave the kingdom without a queen?"

"Well – your father could marry again, my lady. He is not too old to have more children, if you forgive my choice of words."

"So you think I should run away instead of facing this situation and dealing with my problems?"

"No – I'm sorry, my lady. It was a foolish idea."

"Any other ideas then?"

"I think – I think you should follow your heart, my lady. Just be who you are and don't try to hide anything. Then the people will trust you, I'm sure."

"Thank you," Ebony beamed and had to keep herself from rushing forward and giving the maiden a hug. "That is the kind of honest answer I was looking for!"

"I'm glad that I was able to help, my lady. If I may be excused now –?"

"Of course. Thank you."

The maiden hastened away, as if one more second in Ebony's presence might bring her into great trouble. *I guess I have to work on my people skills a bit more, if I don't want to frighten all the people I talk to. But at least she finally told me what she truly thinks.*

The rest of the servants were similarly reluctant to speak to Ebony about the topic of marriage, but she was able to persuade most of them into telling her what they thought of Ebony's love for Viola.

She was relieved to find out that nearly all of them didn't mind having two queens instead of a king and queen, as long as they wouldn't have to worry about anything but their own daily lives and problems.

219

Some mentioned the concern that Ebony and Viola wouldn't be able to have children, but when Ebony told them that they would find a solution so that there would definitely be an heir for the throne, most of them agreed that having two queens wouldn't be too bad.

When Ebony finally returned to her chambers after a long day of walking through the whole castle and talking to any servant in sight, she felt reassured and more confident about her task.

"I can do this," she told herself while brushing her teeth and staring at her own reflection in the mirror. "The people seem to like a happy ending with true love as the winner. Even when the winners are two young women like Viola and I."

Her dark eyes wandered over her pale skin and her red hair. A few curls had escaped her pinned-up hair style and were flowing down her shoulders like a red stream of blood. *I have always tried to live in the shadows, because people didn't like me for who I am. But now it's time to step into the light and show them, that their prejudices were wrong. I'm not a witch, I'm a future queen – one that is deeply in love and willing to risk anything to spend the rest of her life with the one person who loved her from the moment they laid eyes on each other.*

She smiled and pulled the pins out of her hair, letting it flow openly down her shoulders and breasts, covering her white skin with dark red curls. *Viola loves me for who I am. She encouraged me not to hide anymore. And I will return the favour by not hiding my feelings for her. For love isn't something one should have to hide, even if it is as unconventional as ours.*

It was a sunny winter's day when Ebony and her father stepped onto the wooden podium to address the people of their kingdom.

The king spoke first, while Ebony stood behind him, her heart beating so fast that she thought it might jump out of her chest at any moment. *Right now, I would definitely love to take the advice of my maiden and run for it!*

She constantly reminded herself to breathe deeply, but when the king finally handed over to her and stood back, she couldn't help but hold her breath.

Her heart made a leap as she took a few steps forward and faced the waiting crowd. Blood rushed through her ears, so loud that she didn't even hear the soft breeze, gliding over the podium and whistling through cracks in the stone walls nearby. *Don't panic. Stay calm. Breathe!*

She took a deep breath, folded her trembling fingers in front of her and started to speak. At first, it felt like the words were only reluctantly leaving her mouth, as if they were afraid to meet the ears of the stony-faced crowd. But then she remembered Viola's smiling face, kind and loving, hovering before her mind's eye as if she was there to encourage Ebony to do the right thing.

Her words gained new strength and, while holding on to that comforting image of Viola, she spoke more fluently to the people, who suddenly didn't look as grim anymore.

"I know that it is unusual for a kingdom to be led by two queens, but I promise you that we will reign just as kind and fair as any king and queen have done before us. Princess Viola is the most suited person I know to sit on the throne and when it is time for us to leave this world again, we will name a successor, so that you won't have to worry about the throne remaining without an heir."

She paused and looked into the faces in front of her for a few seconds. There were some furrowed brows and doubtful eyes, but she could also see smiles and nods of agreement. *They don't hate me. I can do this.*

"If you want," Ebony continued with an honest smile, "we could even put the succession of the throne to a vote. We could pick a few candidates and let *all of you* choose whom you want as a new ruler."

Astonished silence followed her words, only disturbed by the rustling of clothes and the beat of her thumping heart.

Ebony endured the quiet for a while, resisting the urge to look at her father for comfort. Instead, she faced the people in front of her, trying to read from their eyes what they were thinking about her proposal.

"It is your choice," she finally broke the silence again, forcing herself to keep her voice steady. "You get to decide whether you accept Viola and me as your queens or not. I ask you to raise your hands, if you agree to let me marry the one I truly love and still be your future queen. All those in favour, raise your hand now."

For a split second, no one reacted. It was as if time had frozen, finally succumbing to the bone-chilling cold of winter. Ebony held her breath again, her chest so tight with tension that it felt as if it might break apart.

Then, slowly and reluctantly, the first people raised their hands. *It's working!*

Ebony's heart picked up its speed.

More hands went up into the cold air.

It's really working! They don't hate me and my decision.

More and more people raised their hands, until Ebony was gazing into a sea of smiling faces and raised palms, encouraging her racing heart that it had won its battle.

Her head started to spin, partly due to the lack of oxygen, which reminded her to start breathing again. She took in a few deep gulps of icy air, while a relieved smile spread across her face. *They want me as their queen! And Viola, too! We did it!*

"Thank you," Ebony forced herself to speak again, her voice trembling slightly with excitement and joy. "Thank you for your trust. Now, just to be sure, please put down your hands again and let me ask you: Is there anyone who doubts my decision? Please raise your hand now if you don't want me and Viola to be your queens."

All the people who had raised their hands before took them down again and looked around to see whether anyone would challenge their decision. The seconds crept by with menacing slowness. Ebony's nerves felt like they might rip, but no one raised their hand. No one questioned her decision. She had won.

𝔄𝔣𝔱𝔢𝔯 repeating the nerve-wracking task of asking the people for their consent in every village of their kingdom, Ebony and her father returned to their castle after a few weeks, triumph in their wake.

Much to her own surprise and happiness, Ebony had succeeded not only to make all the people vote in her favour, but even cheer for her and Viola.

Not all the people were thrilled about that news, but none of them openly doubted her decision and some of them had even jubilated and shouted things like "Long live the queens" or "May true love make us stronger".

Ebony was overwhelmed by all the support she got and couldn't help but burst into tears of happiness as soon as she was alone in her chamber again.

"I did it," she sobbed, dancing through the room, a joyful smile upon her lips. "I faced my fears and stepped into the light for all the people to see. And they didn't push me back into the shadows. They didn't condemn me for my choice of love. They accepted it and cheered me on! They like me the way I am!"

She let herself fall onto her bed and stared at the ceiling, imagining how her mother would smile at her with love and fondness in her eyes if she could see her now.

"You always believed in me, mother," she whispered, "and you were right. People will love me for who I am, if I believe in myself and learn to be who I want to be, instead of trying to please the expectations of others."

Her mother's image before her mind's eye smiled, her eyes twinkling with happiness, just like those of her father had done, when he had looked at Ebony on their way home, a fondness on his face that she had never hoped to see. His eyes, too, had been lit up by a smile, like a blue ocean illuminated by the golden light of summer.

Then the vision changed and Viola wandered into Ebony's mind, a dancing embodiment of pride and joy. *She believes in me and our love. I should write to her right away and tell her the good news! She's going to be so excited – very much like I am right now.*

Ebony got up and hurried towards her table, grabbing feather and ink with trembling fingers and started to write a long letter, telling Viola everything that had happened within the last few weeks. Then she dashed out of her chamber to make sure that the letter would be sent to Viola right away, before joining her father in the dining room for a late supper.

"There she is, my heroic daughter, future queen of all my lands – which we'll have to call 'queendom', I guess," he greeted her in a cheerful mood. "Come, let's eat and drink! We have a wedding to plan."

Ebony grinned and quickly joined her father at the table. He hadn't been kidding and started to plan her wedding as soon as she had piled potatoes with rosemary on her plate.

"We have to wait for spring," he mused, "because it would be too dangerous for the guests to arrive during winter – especially when they come from afar, like your fair bride. Or would you prefer a summer's wedding?"

"No, spring is fine," Ebony answered hastily, nearly choking on her potatoes. "I'm sure Viola would love it how all the flowers in the gardens will be in full bloom at that time. And I don't want to get a sunburn during my wedding. Summer and I have never been best friends."

"True. It was Snow White who loved the warmth of summer the most. A spring wedding it shall be then. Do you know what kind of dress you would want to wear?"

"I was actually going to ask Snow White," Ebony admitted reluctantly, blushing a little. "She loves to design dresses. And she never got to see me in the green ball dress she had me made. So I thought she might like to design my bridal gown."

"What a lovely idea! I'm sure she will be delighted!"

They kept talking about Ebony's wedding plans, until sleepiness crept into their minds and reminded them of the demanding weeks which lay behind them.

Before Ebony went to bed though, she wrote a letter to her sister, telling her all about the upcoming wedding. *Not that long ago, I was at her wedding and never would have thought that I myself would get married so soon after. Funny how destiny has its own ways sometimes …*

When she finally went to sleep, her mind was filled by a deep and comforting satisfaction, lulling her senses and letting her glide into colourful dreams, full of happy dancing, laughter and merriment.

$Just$ like Ebony had expected, Snow White was delighted to hear about her younger sister's wedding plans and positively thrilled to get to design the bridal gown.

"You will look like a dazzling dream in white," Snow White exclaimed when she greeted Ebony at her castle two months after their seventeenth birthday for a first fitting. "I was thinking feathers, like a swan, you know? Did you like them on your green ball dress?"

"Yes, I did," Ebony replied with a smile. "The feathers reminded me of snowflakes. Really pretty. And they seemed to look great on me, because that was the evening when I met Viola."

"Perfect!"

Snow White was on fire and dragged her sister into her dressing room to get started right away. Ebony, who had never really enjoyed fancy dresses and sessions with her dressmaker, was surprised how much fun she was having with her older sister, while the latter was bustling about like a busy bee, chatting and singing happily as she did so.

"I got spoiled by my beloved George every day since I've arrived in this wonderfully sunny kingdom here – now let me spoil you a little. Let's see … Diamonds would fit for your chest and hair. And the feathers for the lower part of the dress. We could use silvery feathers this time to make them stand out a little. That way they would match perfectly with the diamonds. Or do you think diamonds would be too much? But they are so sparkly and pretty, like tiny stars. I think a few of them can't hurt. Do you know what Viola's dress will be like?"

Time flew during the visit in Snow White's kingdom and Ebony nearly regretted having to leave her sister again, when she had to return to her father's kingdom to attend the preparations of the spring wedding.

Letters from Viola arrived almost on a weekly basis now and both of them wrote each other poems of love, expressing their joy and excitement for the upcoming events.

'I love you like a summer's breeze,
comforting me with warmth.
I miss you like the buzz of busy bees,
when they flee from a storm.
I love you like the scent of spring,
so lively and so sweet.
I miss you like a bird would miss a wing
and I hope that soon we'll meet.
I love you like the stars above,
which guide me through the night.
I miss you, you're my hearts true love
and soon you'll be my bride.'

Ebony read Viola's last letter again and again, with tears in her eyes and joy in her heart. Those poems and words guided her through the days and weeks of preparation, until the day of celebration finally arrived.

Her father had made sure that it would be a very special occasion, letting the wedding ceremony be followed by the crowning ceremony on the day after.

The people of the kingdom were very excited about both events, looking forward to seeing their future queens getting united and taking over the reign of the soon-to-be queendom so shortly afterwards.

"Are you sure you don't want to be king anymore?" Ebony asked her father repeatedly, while she counted the days until the time she and Viola would be reunited.

"I have ruled this kingdom long enough. I'm tired and getting old. Both my daughters will be married soon. Why shouldn't I retire and enjoy a quiet life as a grandfather?"

"Well, I guess Snow White will have to take care of the latter," Ebony snorted and her father grinned.

"You said that you wouldn't rule out adopting children with Viola once you got married."

"True," Ebony admitted and returned his grin. "But first I'll have to get used to a married life and ruling a queendom, both at the same time. It might take a while for us to think about adopting any other responsibilities."

"I can live with that, as long as you are happy with the choices you make."

"I am," Ebony assured him with a confident smile. "And I will continue to be as long as I choose my own destiny."

And she should be right.

As soon as Viola arrived at the castle, Ebony was in a daze, filled by happiness and relief. She didn't really want to let Viola out of her sight for long, but her father insisted that they would stay apart until the ceremony.

Snow White had outdone herself, creating a special dress for each occasion.

Ebony's wedding gown had been made of floating silk, covered in silver feathers, which made Ebony look like an elegant swan, gliding over the surface of a quiet lake. Viola wore a matching dress, silver with white flowers, like a sea of roses in full bloom. Both she and Ebony had argued that they liked dark red roses better, but Snow White didn't want to hear about it.

"Red for a wedding? That's unheard of! Don't you think you shocked everyone enough by a double-queen-wedding? Do you have to keep breaking with tradition?"

Neither Ebony nor Viola had wanted to argue with that and thus the roses stayed white like snow.

The wedding day itself passed in a blur, followed by a night that exceeded Ebony's wildest dreams of pleasure and joy.

"You know," Ebony whispered, lying in Viola's arms and caressing her naked skin, "I never really thought that I would get married. All the princes only ever cared about my sister. I never thought that I'd be so happy one day, blessed with the privilege to spend the rest of my life with someone as amazing, witty, kind, funny, loving and beautiful as you."

She could hear Viola chuckle, her chest vibrating with amused happiness, making Ebony's head bounce up and down a little.

"Who needs a prince to be happy? Even if I hadn't just met Snow White today," she mumbled and kissed Ebony's head, "I would have had only eyes for you. Your glowing red hair, your fair skin, your breathtaking dark eyes – who can say that you are not as beautiful as Snow White?"

The magic mirror of the evil queen, Ebony thought to herself, but didn't want to talk about the topic right now.

"You truly think I'm beautiful then? Not just because I'm your wife now?"

"Nonsense!" Viola giggled and pulled Ebony closer to her heart. "And who cares about beauty anyway? I would even love you if you were an ugly troll or even a werewolf, because you are the most intelligent and kind-hearted woman I've ever met!"

With those words she made Ebony turn around and look her in the eyes. "And you know what else I love about you?"

Ebony shook her head, even though she knew that the sparkle in Viola's eyes was most likely the fire of lust.

"This."

Viola leaned forward and kissed Ebony so passionately that they were soon entangled in another round of wedding night pleasures and Ebony wished that this night would last a thousand nights.

The day after, the crowning took place under a blue spring sky, where the newly-wed queens looked more radiant than the dazzling sun herself – partly thanks to Snow White's design.

Both Ebony and Viola wore dresses of white silky fabric which was so light that it weaved around them like a summer's breeze with every step they took, making it look like they were floating above the ground. The chest part was embroidered with delicate golden stitching silk, while the lower part of the dress was once more covered with feathers, this time golden, just like the elegant crowns which were put onto both queen's heads.

Ebony was surprised how heavy the crown was, considering the delicacy of its looks. *Appearances can sometimes fool us*, she reminded herself, thinking back to the way everyone had admired the evil queen's beauty.

Then she shook her head and smiled at Viola, who was standing proudly at her side, waving at the cheering crowd. When she felt the gaze of her newly-wed wife upon her, Viola turned and returned Ebony's smile, washing away all doubts and fears which had been left about their future.

I have come a long way from the frightened girl in the green dress with white feathers, who was lost at a ball and found by an angel. And I have yet to keep walking down the path of destiny, growing stronger with every step, so that I will be able to guide this queendom into a better future. But with Viola at my side, I can do it. We can do it. Because nothing is stronger than people who unite in the cause of true love and choose their own destiny.

"**May** they live happily ever after," exclaimed the fairy apprentice with tears in her eyes, while she watched the mirror's image of Ebony and Viola waving at the jubilant crowd of people. "I wish I could be there to bless them and their future."

"Humph," mumbled the Good Fairy while she wrinkled her forehead. "Fairies don't attend weddings. At least not when they are not invited."

"But how are we supposed to get invited if we never show ourselves to the humans?"

"Smart question." The Good Fairy grinned. "We don't."

"We don't what?"

"We don't get invited. Because we are not meant to mingle with the humans. It's not right."

"But what about the stories about fairies blessing the children of kings and queens in other lands? Like Aurora."

"They are just stories."

"How do you know?"

"Because I know the other elders and I know that fairies like to brag at gatherings. That is how the stories are born. It's as simple as that."

"Will you be telling stories about Ebony and Viola at the next fairy gathering?" Arabella asked eagerly, looking back and forth between the image of the mirror and her mistress.

"God forbid! Of course not." The Good Fairy chortled. "No, I will keep this nice and quiet."

"But why?"

"Because the world isn't ready for –"

"– a story with two queens and a happy ending?"

"Exactly," the Good Fairy grumbled. "I was thinking of telling the others the story of 'Snow White and the Seven

Dwarves' instead. Innocent princess, evil witch and a prince who saves the day. That's the kind of story I like."

"Isn't that getting a bit old?"

"*I'm* getting old, why shouldn't my stories do the same?" the Good Fairy snarled, but then steadied herself again. "Alas! You youngsters just don't know how to respect good old tradition."

"Maybe," the young fairy offered, "some traditions are meant to be broken when they are outdated."

"Outdated? Are you calling me outdated?"

"Not you, mistress. Just the tradition of princesses having to marry – or being saved by – princes."

"Do your worst," the Good Fairy sighed. "But I will make sure that the story of Snow White is the one that others will remember."

"Fine." The young fairy raised her chin. "And I will make sure that people will hear about Ebony's story too. We'll see which one they like better!"

Both fairies looked at each other with unbending determination in their blue eyes. And just at that moment the young fairy decided that she would soon start on her own path, as soon as she had mastered the skills of granting wishes – and remembering them correctly.

Even though sometimes a seemingly serious mistake can turn out to be the best thing that has ever happened – both to me and to the queendom.

The End

Acknowledgements

I would like to thank all the wonderful people who have made this fairy tale possible. Because writing can be a lonely process sometimes, but in the end, a lot of people are involved in making the wish of a printed book come true – maybe even a fairy or two …

First, I would like to thank my family, who always support me and make sure that I stay inspired every day. Even during the challenging times of pregnancy and during the first weeks as a mother, I got so much support and love that I managed to finish this book – sometimes writing during the night or writing and breastfeeding at the same time.

I thank my newborn daughter Lara Melina for her unconditional love, endless curiosity and talent to challenge me to change my perspective.

I thank my husband that he took care of our daughter when he was at home, so that I was able to enjoy a few moments of focused writing – and also catch some sleep.

And I thank my parents that they took care of our daughter from time to time as well, so that I was able to finish this book.

Thank you that you all made this possible!

Secondly, I would like to thank the talented designer of my book cover, Carmen (CoverManufakturArt Carmen Schneider), who made sure that the book looks as magical as a fairy tale should be.

I would also like to thank my reader, Hannah (Lektorat Butterblume), who inspired me with her comments and suggestions to make the best of my story.

Then I would like to thank my blogger team for their great support and wonderful feedback. Without you all this book wouldn't have gotten the attention that it deserves and I am very grateful for all your support.

And finally, I would like to thank *you* for reading this book. I am very happy that I am able to share the story of Snow White and Ebony with you and I hope that you enjoyed it.

A huge thank you to all of you and may your wishes always come true!

Michelle Krabinz

Other works of Michelle Krabinz …

"Driving Madness" (2018)

"Die Organ-Chroniken" 1-4 (2018-2020)

"Kampf der vier Elemente 1: Feuer & Wasser" (2019)

"Schriftstellerische Ergüsse" (2020)

"Ehekrise vor der Trauung" (2020)

"Kampf der vier Elemente 2: Luft & Erde" (2021)